T5-DHU-092

SPECIAL MESSAGE TO READERS

This book is published by

THE ULVERSCROFT FOUNDATION

a registered charity in the U.K., No. 264873

The Foundation was established in 1974 to provide funds to help towards research, diagnosis and treatment of eye diseases. Below are a few examples of contributions made by THE ULVERSCROFT FOUNDATION:

A new Children's Assessment Unit at Moorfield's Hospital, London.

•

Twin operating theatres at the Western Ophthalmic Hospital, London.

•

The Frederick Thorpe Ulverscroft Chair of Ophthalmology at the University of Leicester.

•

Eye Laser equipment to various eye hospitals.

If you would like to help further the work of the Foundation by making a donation or leaving a legacy, every contribution, no matter how small, is received with gratitude. Please write for details to:

THE ULVERSCROFT FOUNDATION,
The Green, Bradgate Road, Anstey,
Leicester LE7 7FU. England
Telephone: (0533)364325

VENGEANCE IN HIS GUNS

Brannigan had pursued Lobo for years, swearing to kill him and any Apache who stood in his way. The Indians respected the courage of their white adversary and feared vengeance in his guns. It was only a matter of time before the Indian fighter and the chief came face to face to do battle. Fate brought Brannigan to another who had his own reasons for finding Lobo, and they teamed up to ride into Apache country, to test their courage against the Indians.

VENGEANCE IN HIS GUNS

Brannigan had pursued Lobo for years, swearing to kill him and any Apache who stood in his way. The Indians respected the courage of their white adversary and feared vengeance in his guns. It was only a matter of time before the Indian fighter and the chief came face to face to do battle. Fate brought Brannigan to another who had his own reasons for finding Lobo, and they teamed up to ride into Apache country, to test their courage against the Indians.

PETER TAYLOR

VENGEANCE IN HIS GUNS

Complete and Unabridged

LINFORD
Leicester

First published in Great Britain in 1982 by
Robert Hale Limited
London

First Linford Edition
published July 1992
by arrangement with
Robert Hale Limited
London

British Library CIP Data

Taylor, Peter *1947 Mar. 8 –*
Vengeance in his guns.—Large print ed.—
Linford western library
I. Title
813.54 [F]

ISBN 0–7089–7183–0

Published by
F. A. Thorpe (Publishing) Ltd.
Anstey, Leicestershire

Set by Words & Graphics Ltd.
Anstey, Leicestershire
Printed and bound in Great Britain by
T. J. Press (Padstow) Ltd., Padstow, Cornwall

1

THE clouds moved quickly and the full moon shone in the Arizona sky. The Apache sat cross-legged on the boulder as the night breeze played with the locks of his long black hair. Otherwise he was motionless, watching his two braves snaking their way down the shale ridge to the cabin below.

He saw that his braves had reached the canyon bottom and were lying flat-bellied on a ledge of rock, turning occasionally to look up, watching for his signals to move in. The boy, unaware of the human predators and his eyes not as sharp and accustomed to the gloom as the Apaches, was moving back towards the cabin. There was a click as he entered and the latch-key fell.

The Apache on the boulder remembered this part of the country, for his people had passed that way many times. That was before the White Eyes had come in greater numbers and poisoned it with their presence, forcing his people into merciless desert lands. He remembered when his wife and small son had been at his side. It had not been far from here that he had found his son's body, the scalp torn from the skull. The fate of his wife was still a mystery to him. He could only assume that the White Eyes had taken her and sold her into slavery for he had searched for her body in vain.

Now all was still below, except for the few wisps of smoke drifting from the cabin's chimney. The Apache knew there were only two whites in the cabin, a woman and a boy. He knew too that he would not kill them; he did not make war on women and children. The two braves, like marauding cougars, crept nearer, still watching for his signal, and when it came told them to move in stealthily to take the big white and two other horses.

They sprang into action, leaping from the ledge and landing soft-footed. A coyote bayed to the moon as they ran in a half crouch across the clear ground. Their moccasins kicked up small dust clouds as their bronze bodies slithered under the wooden fence of the corral. The tall brave opened the gate as the other expertly led the first horse through, holding his hands over its nostrils to stifle any imminent protest. Their leader above smiled as the second horse was meekly led out in the same fashion.

Then the tall brave returned again for the prize, the big white the boy had been stroking. Their leader had never seen such a horse, and it put his Indian ponies to shame. This was the horse he had in mind for himself, and he postured what a fine figure he would make astride it and riding amongst the wickiups of his people. The white was more resistant than the others, but the tall Apache's skill with horses prevailed and he soon had it under control.

Suddenly, the incalculable happened. There was the noise of the latch-key being lifted and the sandy-haired boy strode out into the open.

His mouth dropped as he saw what was happening and, up above, the leader saw the three figures freeze simultaneously, statues in the moonlight. Then one of the Apaches galvanised into action, running full speed towards the boy. The youngster had only half turned to run when the Indian reached him, one huge arm encircling his throat whilst the other had closed over his mouth aborting the warning cry before it was given air.

The Apache leader sprang from his perch on the rock and followed his braves' route down the shale ridge. Soon he was beside them in the clearing where the boy was kicking and struggling, but as helpless as a mouse in an eagle's talons.

"Do you not see it is hopeless to struggle," the leader addressed the boy. "An Apache boy would know it."

The command in the voice instantly stopped the boy struggling, but the fear reflected in his eyes. Then there was a voice from the cabin, a woman's, anxiously calling out, "Jimmy! Where are you?"

The leader whispered "Grey Wolf" to the tall brave, and he moved quickly to the door of the cabin so that when the woman came out he grabbed her and dragged her with ease over to the others. He thrust her down into the dust at their feet.

"Woman, where is your man?" their leader asked.

She looked up at him, her pale skin and fair hair even paler and more ghostly in the moonlight and her eyes betrayed recognition.

"You are Lobo," she said, addressing the leader, her voice strangely under control. "I have seen your picture at the fort." Even in the moonlight, the strong jaw line, the flared nostrils and tall thick-set frame marked out this notorious leader of the Apache.

"I am Lobo and it is well that you control your fear. Many could not when I burnt them out."

"What do you want with me and the boy?" Her voice was still clear and steady. "We haven't harmed you. Your quarrels are with the soldiers."

"Do you think Lobo kills women and children?" Grey Wolf made to interrupt but Lobo silenced him with a gesture. He admired the woman, her nerve and self-control.

"I wish only these horses," he said. "We need them to get back." He pointed in the direction of the Dragoon mountains.

"Please leave us the white," she said, asking, but not begging. "Take them all, but leave the white."

"Why should I do this, woman?" The voice was flat and passionless.

"We need him to breed," she explained. "He's a thoroughbred and we're going to start a good horse ranch. It was a dream of ours, my husband and I and the boy." She glanced over at the boy who was still held by the Apache. "My man is dead."

Lobo detected a faint bitterness in her voice for the first time.

Lobo's respect for the woman's coolness tempted him to grant her request but then he remembered his position, chief of the Apache, enemy of the White Eyes. Grey Wolf and Snake Eye were watching him. He would be weak in their eyes if he showed this mercy, and he well knew that his will and reputation as chief depended on a ruthlessness he did not always feel. If these two White Eyes before him had been men it would have been different. They would have been dead by now.

"The horse is mine," he stated. "Your god favours you today. I leave you your house and your boy. I would kill him if he was a little older."

"You'd better kill me," the boy suddenly shouted, freeing his mouth from the Apache's hold. Lobo turned impassively towards him.

"The cub favours his mother," Lobo

addressed Grey Wolf who sniggered.

"That horse was my pa's. He'd have stopped you sure enough if he was alive." The boy was struggling again.

Lobo strode over to him and looked deep into his eyes. He saw courage born of hate, and he knew that if it was an older man looking at him that way, eyes blazing defiance and frustration, he'd have slit his throat. He would not want an enemy like that on his trail, a man who would hunt him ruthlessly. There was already one man like that in his life and he had proved expensive in Apache lives. But he could ignore this young one, for the years would cool him. After all it was only a horse.

Lobo sprang with agility on to the back of the big white and looked down at the group. He signalled his braves to release the two white people and mount up. Then he looked back at the woman and boy, a commanding figure astride the white, powerful thigh muscles gripping its flanks, and sinewy arms holding its mane. The boy, amidst his anger, sensed fully for the first time that night the physical power and presence of a warrior fashioned out of hardship, denial and the animal will to survive in a disappearing age.

"Go to the fort, woman," Lobo said. "You will be safe there for a while. Tell the soldiers Lobo waits for them in the Dragoons. When they come they die."

Then they were gone, spurring their horses into the dusk, a trail of dust in their wake and the boy and forlorn woman staring after them.

"It's not fair, ma," said the boy, first to break the silence.

"I know," she said softly, staring still into the mid distance.

"That was pa's horse before he died and he said that one day he'd be mine too."

"There's nothing to do, Jimmy, nothing to do." The voice was wistful, far off.

"It was the only thing I ever had that was pa's." He stubbed his toe into the ground, stirring dust.

"It's no good talking, Jimmy, no good remembering."

He looked up then, saw the haggard, beaten look on her face and remembered how important the horse had been for their future. A lump rose in his throat.

"I'll get it back, ma," he said resolutely. "I'll get it back."

She looked down at him then, dragging her eyes from the departing figure, ruffled his hair with her hand.

"Never mind, Jim. We'll move away. I'll get a job. Don't worry. This land has been cruel anyway."

The three Apaches rode hard, anxious to reach their camp. An hour after first light they had crossed the desert land and were approaching a high bluff. Suddenly Grey Wolf pulled up and pointed ahead. Lobo saw the wagons encircled under the dipping ledge of the bluff. Whoever it was could have seen them too, so he led his men wide in a loop, before turning back again and approaching the bluff under the cover of some twisted rock formation.

Grey Wolf stayed with the horses while he and Snake Eye used the cover of the rocks to approach the bluff. Their keen eyes picked out the sentries, and eventually they found a spot where they could watch unobserved.

"Scalp-hunters." Snake Eye spat out the word contemptuously.

Lobo remained silent, watching the camp. There were two wagons pulled in against the butte, their canvas pulled back exposing two Gatling guns, their steel barrels reflecting the bright light of the morning sun.

Scattered round the wagons were groups of men, some gringos, some Mexicans and some half-breeds, and here and there, dispersed amongst them, were women of the same kind. Lobo felt Snake Eye pull at his sleeve and followed his pointing finger.

"Chato," snarled Snake Eye as Lobo picked out the figure he was indicating. Hate leapt out of his eyes at first recognition, then he was controlled again, the disciplined Apache.

"Yes, he is their leader. Look how he swaggers." They watched him move from group to group. Lobo puffed out his lips and blew out. "Look how he smiles at them, and yet I can see the poison in his fangs even from here."

Lobo remembered only too well the half-breed Chato who had once been welcome in his camp and shared his fire. But his white blood had shown in the end and he had stolen a knife from one of the Apaches. His crime discovered, Lobo, with the same knife, had given him the ugly scar he wore on his cheek and which branded him a coward and an outcast amongst all Apaches. He had been banished, and watching him now Lobo wished he had killed him.

"When do we clear our land of this nest of vipers?" Snake Eye asked.

"Our chance will come," Lobo stated blandly.

Snake Eye snapped, "It will come

when they have slaughtered most of us. When will Lobo ride against them?"

"Patience, Snake Eye. Why do you think they expose the big guns and post so many sentries? They know we cannot tempt those guns in the open. Our chance will come, but I will not send braves into the mouths of those guns."

"At the forts," Snake Eye replied, "they offer many dollars for the hair of our men, our women and children — any Apache they have not trained like the dog who begs for food. These men hunt us like beasts and live like the scavengers of the desert." His voice was rising. "One day the prey will turn on the scavengers."

"That day will be sweet for me too, Snake Eye, but today we ride away." Lobo turned, and they both stole back to Grey Wolf and the horses.

They mounted up and rode, heading further into the Dragoon mountains. They were picking their way gingerly through some giant cacti when Lobo felt the big white react, not enough for an experienced rider to detect as being abnormal, but sufficient for Lobo to be suspicious. He leapt off its back and motioning to the others to remain crept, half crouched, into the cacti.

He saw what his horse had sensed — a Mexican woman dressed in buckskin and sombrero, her long black hair cascading down her back beneath the sombrero. She was half turned so that he saw her profile and what he saw pleased him — a strong full-lipped face and a sturdy body. He spotted the piebald tethered to the cactus. She was alone.

He stood watching her. She, oblivious to his presence, picked some cacti flowers. Since the day his wife had vanished, he had hardly thought of a woman, but there was something about this one that stirred him. He was a man of quick decision, and seeing the creature serene and graceful he made up his mind that the time had come for him to take a woman again and that this would be her.

He moved towards her slowly to avoid startling the horse. For seconds he stood behind her, almost touching her, the strong aroma of her perfume in his nostrils. Then he grabbed her. She kicked and bit the hand over her mouth until she drew blood, but Lobo held on. It was a mark of her spirit, and he was secretly pleased as he forced her back through the cacti to where the other two waited.

"What is this?" Grey Wolf asked, smiling, amused by the struggle as Lobo bound her hands and tied his headband round her mouth.

"Lobo has found himself a slave," Snake Eye answered, playfully slapping the struggling woman across the rump.

"No!" Lobo turned to them, his face serious. "You are wrong. This one will be Lobo's wife." He watched them closely as he spoke and saw them exchange glances. He knew what they were thinking. Snake Eye voiced it.

"Has Lobo forgotten? It has been

the practice of our tribe only to take Apache women. We are not like other Apache. This will not go well with — " His voice trailed away.

"With my wife's brothers." Lobo finished the sentence for him. "Lobo does not fear them. My wife has been long gone and I fear she is gone forever. Lobo must live for the day, for the moment in these times of trouble."

Neither Apache replied. They were loyal to this man, but each had private thoughts about what would happen when the brothers found out that Lobo had taken a Mexican woman for his wife.

They approached their camp high in the Dragoons round noon. Lobo signalled to the sentry above at the entrance to the canyon.

As they rode in, Apaches stopped their work to stare at them. Lobo knew they were admiring the white horse and were curious about the woman who was slumped across his horse's back, in front of him.

He dismounted at his wickiup, pulled the woman from his horse and threw her inside. A young Apache took his horse and led it away. Grey Wolf and Snake Eye watched all this, and rode off in silence. Several Apaches had by now gathered round, and Lobo faced them.

"The woman is mine. She will be my wife," he stated plainly. "Where are the white men Dog Nose took prisoner?"

A young Apache stepped forward from the crowd. "I will take you to them, Lobo."

The brave led Lobo through the wickiups to the outskirts of the camp where two stakes had been erected. Two white men were tied to these, their arms stretched above their heads and bound to the stakes with rawhide. From the distance they could have been taken as normal human beings, dressed as they were in soldiers' blue uniform. It was only up close that the mutilation performed on their bodies became vivid. Lobo stood a yard from them watching as an Apache took his knife and sliced another strip of skin from the already bloody arm of one soldier. He did it slowly like a craftsman taking pride in his handiwork, a stupid smile sitting on his lips as the soldier screamed a long-drawn-out scream.

Lobo stood nonchalantly watching. If he was given the chance, he told himself, he would do this to every soldier until they left the Apache to their ancient lands. He would torture and burn them until they were driven away as they had driven the Apache to hide from them like the desert insects beneath the sand. He prayed to the gods of the mountain that one day the man they called Brannigan would be a prisoner like the two half humans before him.

He turned his back on the scene and made his way back to his wickiup. As he approached he saw what he had half expected.

Two well-muscled Apaches were standing outside his home, arms folded stubbornly across their chests. One had his leg raised, and under his foot, pressed to the earth, was the Mexican woman. They were his wife's brothers, and the elder one with the greying hair spoke, his words brittle.

"Lobo insults us. The family of his wife."

Lobo studied him and then the other brother.

"I am your chief," he said. "The woman will be my wife. I offer no insult, but you must take this as you will."

"We claim our right," the younger replied.

Immediately, Lobo took one step back and in a quick movement took off his buckskin shirt. Then he drew his knife and moved backwards, bending into a half crouch.

Wordlessly, the elder brother drew his knife and charged headlong at Lobo. It was a clumsy attack for an Apache brave, and the murmurings amongst the gathering crowd confirmed it.

Lobo thrust all his weight onto one foot as if to move off that way and then moved with perfect timing in the other direction. The brother bought the feint and went rushing past. Simultaneously, Lobo's foot shot out like the flicker of a snake's tongue and kicked his opponent below the knee tumbling him into the dust. Then he launched his powerful frame through the air at the prone figure and with a downward, scything movement, buried the blade in the Apache's back until the red blood oozed. He twisted the knife as the Apache's body heaved and then was still. Instinct his spur, he withdrew the knife and leapt to his feet, whirling to face the other brother.

The younger man was more cautious, and drawing his knife faced Lobo, circling him and adapting to each of his adversary's movements like a mirror image. Then they moved, slashing at each other. A quick flash of the blade caught Lobo's chest drawing blood. Again the crowd muttered; this would be a close fight.

The brave struck again, and Lobo parried the blow with his blade, but his timing was fractionally out. Lobo felt a searing pain and saw the top of his thumb hanging loose. He gripped the knife more firmly now, preparing to end it quickly. He was strong in body and would gamble all on a reckless charge that he had scorned in the first opponent.

He drove his legs hard thrusting himself at the brave and grabbing the wrist which held the knife. Fortune favoured him and his enemy went down under his weight. Lobo pinioned him there, concentrating now on releasing his own wrist from the vice-like grip. Suddenly his strength told, plunging his knife downwards again and again. As he rose from the bloodied corpse he spoke to his people. "The gods have favoured me. She will be my wife."

The crowd slowly dispersed in silence,

leaving Lobo standing wide-legged over the dead body. He thrust his wounded thumb between his teeth and bit hard until he felt the flesh and bone in his mouth. He spat it out and thrust his thumb into the flames of one of the cooking fires. He uttered no sound.

He slept for a long time, and when he awoke night was falling. Outside the wickiup he found Yellow Sleeves and Spotted Tail. The latter, though young, had been acting as a scout, and Lobo was anxious to question him about Fort Bowen. They talked, and he learned that Brannigan was at the fort, so he decided to send two more Apaches to try to kill him and take his power. Orders were despatched for the two whom he had chosen. Meanwhile, Spotted Tail stood by waiting, as Lobo deliberated.

"Do I return to the fort?" he asked quietly, shifting his feet, his tone and manner indicating reverence for his chief.

"You have done well for one so

young, Spotted Tail." Lobo's words pleased the young brave. "You will return to the fort for seven more days. Say your farewells and leave when the sun rises."

They left him alone then, and he turned back into the wickiup. The Mexican woman lay, still bound, and now asleep in one corner. She awoke when he untied her, but she uttered no word, staring straight ahead of her with frozen eyes. Pulling her knees up to her chin, she enfolded them in her arms in gesture of withdrawal, yet it was more like resignation as though she was one whom fate had treated badly and she was too ill-used to protest any more. Her features, true, were as appealing as they had been back on the trail, but her eyes told everything.

Lobo spoke firmly. "Were you with the Scalp-hunters, Mexican woman?"

"Yes." Her tone was indifferent.

"Their prisoner?" Lobo questioned.

She sneered in reply. "At first, of course, but you get used to anything in time. You live how you can."

"Who was your man, a Mexican?" Lobo asked.

She sneered again in reply, "Don't flatter yourself that you take me from a Mexican. My man was the leader, a half-breed."

Lobo sprang to his feet. "The gods play tricks that I should take you. You will never be my wife now. My slave, but never wife."

"Chato was his name," she went on, ignoring him. "He will come for me."

Lobo looked hard at her. "I know it. Darkness always returns."

He left the wickiup and wandered through the camp, filled with remorse now for killing his wife's brothers. It had been honourable to kill them in defence of his right to take her as a wife, but for that woman, used by the man he despised, it had been a waste of two good Apaches. He consoled himself with the thought that it might tempt Chato to try something careless.

His thoughts then returned to Brannigan as they often did, and he wondered how long the white man could survive their attacks. Deep down he had a grudging respect for a man who could resist all those attacks — this in spite of the thirty or so Apaches he was rumoured to have killed. He wondered what drove the man. He had heard that he didn't exchange scalps for dollars. What kind of a white man was that — to kill Apaches and not collect rewards? Time, he reflected, might tell.

2

THE boy's mother had been asleep when he had left, and she had not stirred as he had quickly gathered together some of his belongings and scratched out a note explaining his intentions. The note told her he was going to track down the big white and that she must not worry.

He had picked up the trail as the red sun of morning painted the Arizona landscape. His elementary knowledge of trailing kept him on their track, and he was still with it two hours later. But the Apaches had not been careless. They had simply not been worried about the boy following them.

But then he came to a halt where the trail disappeared into thin air, and he realised he had come to the limits of his technique and perhaps of his journey. The Apaches were experts and could mask any trail. It would take another expert to match them. Suddenly the futility of his intentions was brought home full force. They could be anywhere. Wearied by the trail, he decided to rest and to think out his plans.

Spotted Tail's horse had gone lame on the trail, but, undaunted, he had begun to run to the fort. Like many of his kind he was a strong runner, capable of thirty miles without resting, and he had soon fallen into a steady rhythmical running action. Though only a youth who had not yet counted coup, he considered himself a fully fledged Apache and scorned returning to camp to the teasing of the older men.

This was how he came to be on foot and creeping up on the white boy. His sharp eye had spotted Jimmy lying asleep in the shade of some rocks, and now he was within five yards, hand on the hilt of his knife, his intention to count coup. The boy, senses alive, through a half-shut eye watched his predator approaching.

He was two yards away now, his knife out and raised high. Then he was directly over the boy and bringing his knife down. But the boy rolled quickly to his left and the blade stirred the dust as it buried itself to the hilt.

Before Spotted Tail had recovered from the surprise, Jimmy was on his back, one hand round the Apache's throat and the other flailing wildly at his body with all the fury real fear brings.

Though only slightly older than his white adversary, that gap was crucial, and Spotted Tail was more muscled and agile. Gradually, two hands clawing at the restricting arm round his throat, he loosened the boy's grip and flung him into the dust.

Jimmy lay stunned from the force of the landing, his mind a fog in which he searched for clarity, the instinctive will to survive forcing his brain to activate. Seconds passed. Spotted Tail had recovered his knife, and he was poised once again over the boy. Yet at the critical moment the Indian's body froze, his sixth sense awakened to the presence of some other being close by. He could smell white man, and then he was away, running off into the surrounding rocks.

"Keep still, boy," a deep voice resounded as Jimmy's eyes opened. "Don't try to move. Take a spell."

The boy looked up and slowly focused on a lean, unshaven face. It was well worn and weather-beaten and in it a pair of blue eyes danced with a certain impish humour.

"You think this is funny, mister?" the boy groaned as the stranger cradled his head on his arm and gave him a canteen. Jimmy grasped it eagerly and put it to his mouth. The cool liquid slid down his throat, reviving him.

"No, boy, no," the stranger replied. "But you and he were lucky. He must have sensed I was drawing a bead on him to run off so quickly. Only a kid too."

The boy, fresher now, studied his saviour more closely.

"Who are you, mister?" he asked. "Are you a scout or something?"

"Or something?" the man repeated, laughing. "My name is Ben Johnson. What's your handle?"

"Jimmy Davidson."

They shook on it, then the man said, "Come on, let's get a fire going. Some coffee would do you a power of good."

The boy lay back gratefully and watched the man gather some dry cottonwood. Soon a pot of coffee was bubbling and they sat round the fire drinking it.

"Can you read sign, mister? Can you find Apaches?"

"I know a little. Some know more."

"Could you find Lobo, mister?"

"Lobo!" Johnson's eyes lost their humour for the first time. "Hoped I'd never hear that name again."

"You after him too?" the boy asked

eagerly. "Do you want to kill him?"

Johnson looked off into the distance but unseeing as though remembering something.

"No, boy, I don't want to kill him. Why do you ask?"

"I just want my horse back."

"Paches got him, uh?"

"Yep."

Johnson looked away again. "Funny meeting you," he said, "I've just left someone who wanted Lobo so bad he'd kill the whole Pache nation to get to him. Now I meet you. Pretty special horse, uh?"

The boy nodded assent. "Who's this man who wants, Lobo?"

Johnson supped his coffee and looked into the distance as he spoke.

"A friend — a former friend of mine," he corrected himself. "Stood as much as I could. I was sick of his blood-lust and watching the hate eat out of his innards."

"Your best friend?" the boy interjected.

"That's right, boy. My best friend.

His wife was killed by Lobo, or so he says. They raided his home while he was away."

"Why didn't you stay with him? Seems a friend should do that no matter what." The boy's face was grave, and the man laughed ironically.

"You're right, of course, but you see one day, I realised he didn't want me any more — didn't want nobody no more — just wanted to kill Paches." Johnson paused. "Why are you asking anyway?"

"What's his name?" the boy questioned.

"Brannigan — Jim Brannigan. Why the interest?"

"Maybe he'll help me."

Johnson laughed again, cynically this time. "Help you? He can't help himself any more. If I was you I'd head right home, wherever that is."

"I'm set on getting my horse."

Johnson detected the determination in the boy's tone.

"Brannigan's at Fort Stanton."

"Guess that's the way I'll head."

Johnson's eyes narrowed. "Of course, you know all about Apaches and their methods. If they catch you they sure go to town. Got all sorts of ways of killing. Heard once how the Lypans buried six soldiers up to their necks amongst some ant-hills. The ants weren't hungry that day."

"How many Apaches has Brannigan killed?" Jimmy refused to be put off.

"'Bout thirty all told, and they still come. Lobo sends two at a time to get him. Mark of respect. They try to take him, and he kills 'em. I stood as much as I could living like that. One day they'll get him dead or alive. I hope it's dead for his sake."

The conversation ended with the going down of the sun, and in silent consent they settled for the night.

"Will he come back?" The boy spoke into the enveloping darkness, remembering now in the half oblivion of approaching sleep how near he had been to death.

"Naw! He was just a boy, probably on some kind of initiation. Go to sleep."

The boy turned over, and his thoughts revolved to Brannigan. In the morning he would set off and seek him out.

When Jimmy awoke at the first sign of light Johnson was already up, and seeing the boy awake brought him a plate of beans. They got to talking again.

"I'm going back to the fort," Johnson announced. "Think I'll give him another chance. Help him to see it through if I have to. Our talk last night made me think. You can ride with me if you want."

The boy was pleased as they saddled up, mounted and rode. They had not gone many miles when Johnson signalled a halt. "Sandstorm coming," he grumbled, peering into the distance. "Best get off and walk the horse, boy."

So they walked on, Johnson leading,

as the first hints of the storm hit them from the north-west. Then it came, full blown, a huge orange cloud that covered the sun. They pulled their hats low and plodded on, each step requiring a giant effort. Suddenly, like a baby hushed from crying, it stopped and it was clear ahead. Johnson lifted his head from his chest, wiped the dust from his clothes and undid the bandana from his mouth.

He saw them first and froze.

"It's cleared up. I — " The boy's words leapt back down his throat as he too saw them. Six Lypan Apaches on horses, statue still, watching them from a sandy ridge.

"Don't move, boy." Johnson's voice was sharp.

The boy looked at him, at the Lypans, and back again at Johnson.

"Are they friendly, Ben? Are they from the fort?" He fought down the panic in his voice.

"No, and we can't run either. They're too near."

Both whites waited, the boy realising the extent of the danger, the man watching, his hand itching to take his Spencer from its scabbard.

Johnson saw the war paint on their faces and the war arrows they carried. No mistake. This was a full-blooded war party, but there was one slight chance.

"Are the Lypans afraid of the clear day that they sneak in the tail of the cloud?" he shouted sneeringly. "Who is the leader of these mighty warriors?"

One of the Apaches, the one in the red shirt, urged his horse forward in silent answer. Johnson saw the fresh scalps on his belt.

"Does it take six Lypans to hunt a man and a boy? Does their leader Ugly Dog, whom I recognise, fear to meet a White Eye alone in combat? Is he such a squaw?"

Ugly Dog laughed loudly, showing a set of broken teeth.

"I do not need to prove myself. I am known as a warrior." He laughed, turning to his braves for their approval, but seeing immovable faces and knowing that in his village that night they would tell how he refused the challenge of the White Eyes. His reaction was decisive. He leapt from his horse, drawing his knife.

"Come, white man, and die." Ugly Dog crouched forward, waiting. Johnson drew his own knife. The boy watched in horror, knowing that words were useless.

Then they were together, circling and slashing. The Apache tried all he knew, and then resorted to the old, well-used trick. Dropping to one knee, he scooped up a handful of dirt and hurled it in Johnson's face. The white man dropped his guard momentarily, and Ugly Dog was on him, knocking him down, and then his knife was against Johnson's throat so that he could not move.

The waiting Apaches screamed their victory, and one of them spurred his horse down the ridge and seized the bridle of Jimmy's horse.

Ugly Dog pulled Johnson to his feet. The knife was in his back now. One of the other Apaches pulled the boy from his horse, and he and Johnson were bound hand and foot with rawhide thongs. Ugly Dog stood over them smiling. "They will die slowly," he announced.

Jimmy could feel cold sweat running down his spine as physical fear swept through his system like a wave of nausea. Johnson said nothing, but resignation was written on his face. He was preparing himself for what lay ahead and this communicated itself to the boy.

They watched the Apaches build a fire which they sat round, smoking and drinking mescal. This went on and on, but, finally, one Apache, bleary eyed from the mescal, staggered towards them and stood over them leering.

"The old one first," Ugly Dog shouted over from the fire, and the Apache freed Johnson. The rifle in his back forced him to where the others sat.

The boy was terrified by what happened next. It was his first encounter with the real depths of savagery which was part of the Apache way. Life to them was a cheap commodity to be used up like water.

They dragged Johnson to the fire and laid him down so his head was almost in it. Then they tied his arms to stakes to secure him. The boy saw Johnson's body arch in natural resistance but he did not cry out. Even though he must have known what was coming, he endured thus far stoically.

The braves squatted round the fire and built it up slowly, guffawing all the time, until the heat at Johnson's head grew unbearable. Still he did not cry out. The flames were licking the air round his head, and the boy twisted in terror as he saw them at last reach their intended destination. The piercing scream, always imminent, rent the air as the fire did its job. It went on for an eternity — loud animal noises. Then there was a low whimper and it was silent. The boy opened his eyes and waited, saying a silent prayer.

Ugly Dog came for him. He untied the bands and forced the boy to his feet. He could smell the Indian, and even this close to death it revolted him. Ugly Dog pushed him to the ground next to Johnson, and they all laughed as he was forced to look at the inhuman head.

They were tying his arms to the stake when there was a high-pitched whistle which ended with a thud near one of his arms. The arrow vibrated as all the Lypans turned to look at it.

They were dumbfounded. The green twine around the shaft told them it was a Chiricahua war arrow.

They turned in unison and looked into the sun. The boy lifted his head and saw the arrow's source.

On the sandy ridge above, two figures were outlined, a man and a horse with the sun behind them so that they fused into a single image. In his hand was a bow. The horse pawed the ground — otherwise the image was still, waiting.

"Lobo," one of the Apaches eventually cried out in recognition. "He warns us."

"We must leave this time," another announced. "He will have more braves with him."

They moved away from the fire and the boy, their eyes never wavering from the figure on the ridge. There was no hurry to their movements. They were humiliated enough without that. Though Apache, Lobo was not of their tribe, their kind. So far they had avoided contact with his band and this was how they wished it — his force was superior to theirs.

They rode off, and the boy watched them go wondering what kind of trick fate was playing. Had he simply exchanged one set of circumstances for another equally as dangerous. He tried to get up but found the rawhide too tight. He pulled and tugged in desperation, glancing up intermittently at the shadowy figure, expecting any moment the high-pitched whistle which would announce his death, but it did not come.

He saw the horse start down the sandy ridge, coming out of the sun, looming larger every second as he struggled with the rawhide. Then, slowly, he was aware of the dark shadow cast on the ground around him. He stopped struggling and looked up, his face suddenly registering surprise and then resignation. It was Lobo who sat on his white horse looking down at him. He felt strangely cool and ready for death. The bow could provide a quick release, far better than the long-drawn-out affair he had witnessed.

Lobo brought one thigh across the horse's back and slid down. Their eyes met briefly. Lobo saw not the hate of the previous night, but resignation, the kind of look he had seen in a trapped animal. His knife was quickly out and cutting the boy free.

The boy, unbelieving, rubbed his wrist as Lobo sprang back onto the white. A whistle brought another Apache over the ridge and down to join them. Lobo made a sign indicating he should dismount. This he did and leapt up behind Lobo. A long look passed between Lobo and the boy before Lobo wheeled the horse and rode off. The boy watched him go, amazed at the turn of events. Lobo could have killed him, but had refrained as on the previous occasion. What kind of man was he?

He waited, regaining his nerve and composure and then mounted up on the horse they had left him.

The sun beat down on his head as he kept going, heading for the fort. He thought of Johnson and wondered if he had any relations or friends at the fort. He did not relish the thought of telling them how he had met his death.

Once he looked back along the trail and saw the buzzards gathering. He realised he should have buried Johnson, and found it hard to forgive himself for not doing so. Pure fear was his excuse.

He had confused thoughts about Lobo. He was puzzled and grateful, but at the back of his mind he knew that whatever happened he must be resolute in his plans to retrieve the white. Brannigan would be the man to see.

3

FORT STANTON was situated at the head of a rocky valley with a steeper slope to the east. It consisted of headquarters, adjacent officers' quarters, three bunk-houses, stables, a supply store, an arsenal and several civilian living-areas. All the buildings were timber except for the arsenal which was made of adobe. To the west was a small trading-post and an Indian agency.

The boy rode in, dusty from his ride, taking it all in. On a square which served as a makeshift parade ground, a sergeant was drilling some new recruits, and the boom of his voice echoed round the fort.

The boy hitched his horse outside one of the bunk-rooms for enlisted men and mounted the board-walk. A soldier, the boy noticed was a captain, was approaching. He stopped, lit a match on the sole of his boot, and cupping his hands put it to a cigar. The boy decided to ask him about Brannigan.

"Scuse me, sir."

The captain heard the voice, shook out the match and turned his attention to Jimmy, who, seeing the sour, hard-bitten look on his face, wished he had picked someone else.

"Yes," the captain snapped, and the boy thought it best to get straight to the point with this man.

"Can you tell me where to find Jim Brannigan?"

The man's face became even more unpleasant and he took out his cigar and spat. "Whad you want him fer?" he asked rudely.

"With respect, sir, that's my business."

The captain's small, close-together eyes studied him more closely. "Please yourself," he replied sourly, but from the look of him the boy was glad he was not more abusive. "That sidewinder is somewhere about. I smell him." He twitched his nostrils in mockery, and there was a long silence while the captain weighed the effect of his words.

"Why don't you like him, mister?" the boy asked, again coming straight to the point. "What did he do?"

"Do? That's the trouble, kid — didn't do anything. Knows the country and 'paches better than anybody but won't do nothing to help us." The man spat the words out, staccato fashion, shaking his head from side to side.

Disliking the man and realising that little help would be forthcoming, Jimmy moved on.

Outside one of the civilian houses, a middle-aged, grey-haired woman was sitting reading. He stopped and cocked his head to one side to see what book she had. He read out loudly, 'The Savages of the West. A Study of a godless people. By R. C. Dangerfield.'

Hearing his voice, the woman slammed the book shut and pulled the shawl further round her shoulders. She looked at him primly over her spectacles, with piercing blue eyes.

"Scuse me. Looking for Jim Brannigan. Can you help me?" the boy said, stepping back.

"Brannigan?" she repeated. "The devil hisself you're after, boy, and I wouldn't help you find the devil. He'll find you in his own good time. Go away, boy, and take the devil's name with you."

He moved on again, this time to the building which had the sutler's signpost above it. A fat man in a white coat was busy outside.

"Got any guns?" Jimmy asked.

The man stopped, eyed him up and down and nodded affirmation. "Go in," he said. "I'll be with you in a minute. Just finish ma chores."

The boy entered the store. It was gloomy inside, the only light coming from a broad shaft through the open doorway. A lamp was lit in one corner to compensate, and the boy's eyes, still not focusing well, picked out vague shapes which looked like rifles stacked in a corner.

He moved to inspect them, cautiously to avoid the barrels and racks strewn about the room.

When half-way across he felt his foot kick something on the floor, and a voice groaned making him start back in surprise.

A large shape, an incomprehensible mass in the gloom, hauled itself from the floor, and the boy stood back watching it stagger towards the light. Jimmy saw the outline of a jug in one hand as the figure moved out of the gloom until a broad back was silhouetted in the faint light.

The man, for that much was discernible, flopped a limp hand, the free one, on the counter and lounged forward. Then, making an effort, he raised the jug to his mouth, threw back his head and gulped the liquid down. Jimmy heard the throb as the whisky galloped down his throat.

Slowly, the man turned to face the boy, but the latter was only aware of the large bulk, the face still masked by the darkness.

"That you, Jake? Gonna kick me out?" His speech was slurred and his figure swaying.

The boy took a tentative step forward until he could smell the whisky fumes. "It ain't Jake," he said, unsure of himself.

"Ain't Jake?" the figure said. "Ain't Jake?" he repeated stupidly, and turned clumsily, supporting himself on the counter.

He stood there a full minute, the boy's eyes still fixed on him, and then slowly, like a snake coiling up to rest, slid to the floor, unconscious.

The boy, thinking he might be hurt, moved into the light and bent over him. The smell of the whisky and a mixture of stale sweat and tobacco tormented his nostrils as he tried to prop up the man's body. He saw the face, clearer now, in the stronger light.

It was broad-featured and topped by a mass of straight long yellow hair tied with a band, Apache-style. A thin scar ran down part of the left cheek. He would not have called the man ugly, but neither would he have called him handsome; world-weary would have been the best description.

The dim light suddenly grew dimmer, and the boy turned. The fat man in the white coat stood in the doorway, blocking it.

"He drunk again," he offered, coming forward and moving the boy aside. "Wish he'd pick somewhere else to get drunk." He waddled over to a barrel, ladled some water out and, bending over, threw it in the drunk's face. The head rose slowly from its hanging position and the eyes sprang open, like traps suddenly released, and a pair of sky-blue eyes stared out at the two hovering over him, before shutting again.

"Help me get him up, will you, boy?" the storekeeper said. "He'll just sleep all day if I don't get him out front."

They hauled and pulled the man to his feet and manoeuvred the huge bulk to the open doorway. They got him outside, and he groaned and shielded his eyes from the light as they propped him against the wall. This time he slid voluntarily to the floor of the board-walk.

The fat man dusted himself down. "Okay. Thanks. Now that we've dealt with Brannigan, what can I get you?"

"Brannigan!" The boy's voice was incredulous as he stared down at the drunken, unkempt figure.

"Sure, boy. Jim Brannigan. Know him?"

"Er — yes," the boy half lied. "I'll — I'll come back tomorrow for my goods, mister. Think I'd better take Brannigan home if he has a home."

"Lives in a boarding-house run by a woman name of Rosie Cutter, a widow woman." The fat man pointed out a low building. "She's Irish. Only one that'll let Brannigan into a house."

Jim turned his attention to Brannigan. He was struggling to get him upright, and the storekeeper gave him some help.

"That's his horse," the latter announced, pointing out the animal at the hitching-rail.

The boy followed the man's pointing finger and saw the horse. But it was the saddle which really drew his attention, not because it was unusual, but because, hanging from it like dark funeral drapes were bunches of black hair — Apache scalps. The boy shuddered.

Somehow they lifted Brannigan's limp form across the horse's back. Thanking the man and leading his own and Brannigan's horse, Jim made his way towards the widow's house.

It was a simple affair, as unpretentious as all the rest of the living-quarters in the south-west forts at that time. The boy rapped on the door, and a woman opened it. She was homely-looking, auburn hair showing the first signs of grey, but still pretty though the boy guessed she had seen better days. Her green eyes inspected the boy and the horse, and her eyebrows rose when she saw Brannigan, crinkling her forehead.

"Mercy!" she exclaimed, the green eyes flashing angrily. "That's the third time this week. Help me get him inside."

Another struggle took place, but the woman was hardier than the boy expected and they got Brannigan inside and put into a cot in the back room. The boy helped her to take off Brannigan's boots.

"Off into the other room, boyo," she said as she dabbed Brannigan's forehead with some cool water. "There's some coffee on the stove. You'll probably need it after heaving this carcass."

Jim helped himself to the coffee as the woman suggested and sat in the big rocking-chair next to the stove. The woman soon joined him and pulled up a chair for herself.

"Now," she said, sitting back, "where've you come from and where'd you find that no good Brannigan?"

"I've come to ask Mr Brannigan to help me find Lobo," he told her straight out, and went on to recount the story of the white horse and the happenings on the trail.

"So Johnson's dead," she said with sad eyes when he had finished. "It'll hit Brannigan hard. Is it worth it, dear? Haven't you had enough of Lobo?"

"'Tis, ma'am. It's worth a lot to me and ma."

She nodded her head slowly in agreement. She could see from the grim expression in his eyes, so like the one she often saw in Brannigan's, that it was no use arguing.

"Brannigan might help," she replied. "Take some persuasion though."

"Johnson said he probably wouldn't."

"He might if we both try. You see, Brannigan and I are fairly close. He was a good man before his wife died, and I can still see a little good in him though he can be as mean as a black sky over the mountains of Mourne."

She rose from the chair and walked over to the window. The boy decided he liked her — liked her sympathetic nature.

"It's getting dark," she announced. "You'd better stay here tonight. You can tell Brannigan tomorrow."

He readily agreed, feeling the weariness of the trail in his bones, and she led him to a small room. When he was in bed she came in and turned down the light and wished him a good night.

He slept well, but in his dreams that night, a lone Apache warrior sat astride a big white horse, watching him.

Next day, the woman and boy were eating breakfast when Brannigan emerged. He ignored them as he strode over to the table, sat down, and began tucking in to the eggs the woman had placed before him. Eventually, rolling the eggs round in his mouth, he spoke.

"This the feller who helped me last

night?" He jerked a thumb at Jim.

The woman looked across at the youngster. "Yes, and you should be mighty grateful the state you were in," she replied.

"What's he after then?" the Indian fighter said in a sneering voice which embarrassed the boy, bringing colour to his face.

"By the saints, Brannigan." The woman was colouring too, but with temper. "Not everyone's after something." Then she looked down at the tablecloth as Brannigan's blue eyes turned on her. "Well," she said sheepishly, "as a matter of fact he wants some help getting a horse back."

Brannigan drew in his breath and let it go. "I ain't got no time to ketch horses, Rosie."

"Lobo stole the horse, Ed," Rosie said softly in reply, as the boy, watching Brannigan's face change, saw an almost imperceptible wince.

"Lobo!" His voice, in contrast to

the woman's, was as cold as ice. He stopped eating. Then he suddenly gathered himself again. "That doesn't really surprise me though. Steals horses all over Arizona."

"But this one's different, Ed. Special to the boy," she explained, and went on to tell him Jim's story, while Jim sat weighing up Brannigan. Then Brannigan chipped in.

"But how can I help him anyhow, Rosie? I don't know where Lobo holes up — stupid to take a boy out there."

"I can show you where I saw him last," the boy announced.

Brannigan laughed cynically at that, annoying the boy. "'Paches are like the wind, here one minute, gone the next. Some of them I find sure enough but mostly they're harder than fleas to catch, especially Lobo, and they make you scratch if they ketch you first."

The boy's disappointment showed in his face, but the woman had softened Ed up a little and he tried again. "Can I ride out with you, Mr Brannigan? At least give it a chance."

But Brannigan shook his head. "Waste of time," he snapped. "You'd hold me up out there."

The boy stared hard into Brannigan's eyes, again annoyed by the coolness and indifference he saw there. "Johnson was right," he said, contempt riding on every word as he turned away.

"Johnson?"

"Yes, Ben Johnson. Rosie left that part out cos she didn't want to hurt you. I won't leave it out. Johnson was the man on the trail and he died coming back to help you."

"Damn." Brannigan's fist hit the table, shaking the plates and cutlery.

"Yes, Mr Brannigan," the boy went on, "and he told me the reason he left in the first place because you weren't interested in nobody but yourself."

"The boy's right, Ed," the woman added. "You can't go on this way. The boy's dead set on getting his horse, and he'd be safer with you. You know how to survive."

There was a long and ominous silence. Brannigan got up and took the dishes over to the sink.

"Okay," he finally said. "I'll take you, boy. Maybe Ben would have wanted that, but that's the only reason. If you foul up, we're both dead."

"I'll be all right," Jim said, and silence fell again.

Then, as the woman rose to clear the table, a rifle-shot rang out, followed by others. Brannigan grabbed the woman and boy and ushered them into the back room as the drumming of hooves grew louder and louder. Then they stopped for a second and there was a loud thud against the door of the cabin. The drumming resumed again and then faded slowly into the distance. Brannigan rose from the floor.

He was standing at the open doorway as Rosie and Jim emerged. A long Apache war lance and a tomahawk were embedded in the wooden door. Brannigan was looking down the road to the soldiers lying in the dust, probably dead. It was with anger he pulled out the lance and broke it over his knee.

"They had a damned cheek riding in here," he said, speaking to nobody in particular.

"What does it mean?" Rosie inquired as Brannigan turned back to them.

"It's a challenge," Brannigan replied. "It means two more will be coming after me. That's their way of letting me know it." He looked at Rosie and the boy. "I'd better pull out right now, Rosie," he said. "They might come right in here after me." Rosie nodded agreement as Brannigan turned to the boy. "You be ready in half an hour," he said unenthusiastically.

The boy was as good as his word, and half an hour later they were ready for the trail. The woman had packed them some hard tack and beans. Brannigan had collected his bedroll and ammunition. As they rode off Rosie called out, "Come back safe — the two of you."

The boy did not take a lot of notice of the tame Apaches squatting in a group round one of the timber buildings, until one of them turned around. The surprise made him draw rein.

"What's the matter, boy?" Brannigan asked, reining in next to him. "Got cold feet already?"

"Naw, Brannigan," he replied, "just thought I saw somebody I knew."

He did not know why he had not given Spotted Tail away and Spotted Tail couldn't figure it either. They had recognised each other instantly.

Then as they rode on out of the fort, Jim suddenly knew why. He was giving Lobo back an Apache life for his own.

Brannigan broke the silence first. "You sure it was Lobo saved you, boy? Never known an Apache show any mercy — a bunch of 'em killed a little girl at Taos two weeks back — bashed her brains out agin some rocks."

The boy nodded, "I'm sure."

They were silent again, the boy leading, as they crossed the desert land heading for the Dragoons and the spot where Jim had last seen Lobo.

But they were only three miles out when Brannigan halted and sat staring ahead. The boy stopped too, but could see nothing.

"What is it?" he asked, but Brannigan ignored the question and raised himself in his stirrups to get a better view.

"Dunno what it is," he said finally. "Just got a sense something was wrong. Thought I saw a movement up ahead." He pointed to some mesquite in the distance.

They spurred their horses forward once again, but the boy sensed that Brannigan was more alert now, his hands poised higher on the reins, restricting his horse a little more.

They were fifty yards from the mesquite when the shot rang out. Brannigan, as quick as lightning, pushed the boy off his horse and leapt out of the saddle himself, at the same time pulling the reins of his own horse hard so that its legs buckled and its body fell. When the second shot came he had already floored the boy's mount in the same way, and now they lay behind their respective horses.

The boy wiped the dust from his mouth as Brannigan took the Spencer from its scabbard and pivoted it on the saddle of the prone horse. He took out his colt and handed it to the boy. "Just in case," he said.

The boy peered over his horse but saw nothing except flat ground ahead. Then another shot rang out singing over their heads.

"Wild shooting," Brannigan muttered.

"Can you see 'em?" the boy asked, but Brannigan was already drawing a bead on the mesquite.

"I can't see anything," the boy said, seeing Brannigan's trigger-finger tightening.

"Watch five yards left of the

mesquite," Brannigan suggested, his eyes fixed ahead.

Then another shot came, and Brannigan's rifle followed it close enough in time to be an echo of the first, but far deadlier than its forebearer. The boy, watching where Brannigan had indicated, saw a figure rise out of the sand, stagger sideways like a drunk, and collapse in a heap. Overhead, a buzzard, which had been circling, moved in close.

"They've dug into the sand," Brannigan said, ejecting the spent cartridge. "Covered their blankets with sand."

"Brannigan!" An Apache's guttural voice boomed, followed by another shot well off the mark.

Brannigan grinned. "They can't shoot," he said. "That's an old one-shot rifle. I'll rush him after the next one."

The next shot hit the dust in front of the horses. Instantly, Brannigan leapt to his feet, issuing a yell as bloodcurdling as any Apache's, and started running, firing his Spencer from the hip.

The boy saw the Indian rise out of his hole and fumble with his gun while Brannigan kept right on running, whooping and hollering as he went. Then he pulled up twenty yards from the Apache. The Spencer came up and he took slow deliberate aim. There was a report, and a slug knocked the Apache flat on his back as it tore his jawbone away.

When Jim reached him with the horses, Brannigan was taking the scalps, and the boy heard them pop. He turned away in disgust.

4

THEY rode steadily towards the mountains. The change in Brannigan amazed the boy. Back there at the fort he had been a two-bit bum, a kind found regularly in any town in the south-west. But out there, in the wild, his accustomed environment, he was a different man, keen-eyed, alert and tall in the saddle. His efficiency in dealing with the Apaches, the cruel scalpings apart, had impressed the boy.

It was round noon when they neared the spot where Jim had last seen Lobo. Nearby they could see the foothills of the Dragoons. They topped the sandy ridge down which Lobo had come riding, and the ground fell away. Brannigan's keen eye picked out Johnson's mutilated form half covered. It took them a half-hour to bury him, and then they rode on, Brannigan in sombre mood.

They found the remains of a fire about a mile from the foothills, and Brannigan dismounted to inspect the camp-site.

"Dry chippings," he announced, turning some horse dung with a stick. "They left this morning." He walked over to some horse tracks. "That way," he said, pointing to the Dragoons.

The tracks indeed led them into the foothills and then the mountains. Lobo though, if he had known, would have been only a little concerned for he had other matters at hand as he and his men watched two figures on horseback, carefully progressing along the rocky surface of a canyon bottom, the hard sound of the hooves echoing intrusively against the steep walls. Lobo waited as the two drew nearer and then signalled the mounted Apaches to follow him down.

They picked their way gingerly over the rocks, down the side of the canyon, their ponies' hooves already wrapped in cloth so that no sound could betray them.

The thin worried-looking Mexican looked up at the walls and rocks ideal for an ambush, and wiped the sweat from his brow, regretting his greed-inspired mission. He did not like this place. It was too quiet — as silent as a graveyard in the town of Sonora from which he had come. He wanted to find Lobo, but hoped he would have the chance to arrange a proper safe trade before Lobo found him.

He plodded on, leading the second horse behind him. The proud-looking Apache woman who sat it, hands bound securely behind her back and feet tied under its belly, craned her neck to view the canyon walls. She knew too it would be a good place for Lobo to attack.

The Mexican's horse reached softer ground, and he felt safer than on the hard rock where it was difficult to get up speed. But this was small consolation when he heard the savage cries behind and turned to see the band of Apaches eating up the space between them. His quirt lashed down on his horse and he jerked the woman's horse after him.

They rode fast and hard to outrun the menacing dust-cloud behind them, and the Mexican could hear his heart thumping, feel it leaping. His sombrero streamed behind him in the wind. The fact that Apaches hated Mexicans more than gringos and if they caught him there would be hell to pay, lent him wings.

He assessed his chances and was confident that he had two good horses built for speed, while the Indian ponies, though slower, were hardy animals and probably had more stamina. His horse would inevitably tire first in a long chase, and the relentless cloud behind would gain on them. Moreover, he knew that Apaches never gave up when they scented a hated Mexican. He decided that hit-and-run tactics might work. His only other choice was to simply turn and face them, hoping that they were Lobo's men. Perhaps the return of the woman would save his life. But he soon realised the foolishness of his last thought and dismissed it.

His decision made, he reined in pulling sharply at his horse's bridle and turning it and the woman to face the Apaches. The Sharps came up to his shoulder and the first bullet knocked an Apache clean off his horse and backwards, arms splayed wide. There was a faint slowing up of the Apache band, and then the second bullet found its home, knocking another Apache from his horse as it tore away his windpipe. Wary now, they reined in and the Mexican pumped more bullets into them, the time expended giving his own horse time to gain renewed strength.

He peppered them for a full minute, throwing them into confusion, and then, taking full advantage, spun his own horses and drove them into a hell-for-leather sprint.

The woman turned in the saddle, saw the Apaches gather, compose themselves again, and the dust rising as they kicked their horses into pursuit.

They had sprinted a half-mile before the Mexican repeated his delaying tactics, but this time, the Apaches, wiser now, spread themselves wider and kept coming. The Mexican panicked and started the horses running again using the quirt on their already lathered backs in an effort to squeeze the last ounce of strength out of them.

They had run over a mile through the canyons, and the Apaches had gained all the time until they were within a hundred yards. The Mexican was crossing himself and mumbling a prayer, expecting at any moment the sharp searing pain of an arrow in the back. But it did not come, and then, suddenly, his prayers were answered.

Through the stinging sweat running from his brow into his eyes he saw his saviours — two canvas-covered wagons rumbling towards him with riders accompanying them.

He spurted as the two wagons drew apart to let him through and then turned side on to the approaching Apaches. The Mexican reined in, saw the canvas tops lifted and heard the rat-tat-tat of two Gatling guns.

Apaches and horses hit the ground together in the first murderous volley. Lobo saw the carnage around him and signalled the retreat. The remaining braves fell back to a safe distance, and Lobo rode out in front of them, riding his horse up and down peering at the guns which had meted out such punishment, his heart full of anger.

A figure came out from behind the wagons and even at that distance he knew it was Chato who was waving his rifle above his head in confident gesture of triumph.

The chief yelled, "Laugh loud and long, Chato, but I, Lobo, have your Mexican woman for my slave."

The bullet Chato fired in reply fell

short, for Lobo had judged the distance perfectly.

Chato went into the shelter of the wagons again, leaving Lobo and the remnants of his band hovering in the distance. He turned his attention to the newcomers. The Mexican was facing him, but the woman's back was to him.

"Buenos Dios, hombre," Chato said. "You were lucky, eh?"

"Yes, señor," the Mexican replied. "You came from God."

Chato laughed loud at this, and the Mexican didn't like it. It was a laugh the irony of which spoke louder than words.

A fat Mexican with a pock-marked face and an eye-patch over one eye strutted over to inspect them. He stood next to Chato, listened to him laughing and then whispered in his ear, "Why do we wait, amigo? Kill this fellow and let's see what he has with him." He smiled up at the Apache woman's back as he spoke.

"Do not be so hasty, Garcia," Chato said. "There's plenty of time."

But already One Eye had drawn his knife and was fingering the blade, his mouth lolling open stupidly as he studied the newcomers.

Chato saw this. Immediately his face contorted with rage and he struck out at Garcia, hitting him full on the mouth, knocking him down.

"I'm boss, see," he said as Garcia, nursing his jaw, searched the dust for his broken tooth. "What I say you do plenty quick."

One Eye picked up his sombrero and struggled to his feet. The Mexican on the horse, wondering what it was all about, watched him shuffle and shamble away. Chato turned back to him and gave him a gleaming ingratiating smile.

"Just a little argument," he offered. "Now, señor, where are you heading?"

The Mexican thought quickly, anxious to protect his interest, the Apache woman.

"My squaw and I are heading for Fort Stanton," he explained, his throat dry, "to visit one of my wife's relatives."

Chato smiled again and looked up at the woman's back.

"Want to show me your squaw, uh?" he said patronisingly so that the Mexican did not dare to refuse.

The Mexican nodded and obeyed, pulling the woman round.

Chato's face registered surprise, then an evil humour as he smiled up at the woman. She looked down at him, her eyes clearly spelling out hate. Chato turned to the Mexican. "You lie well," he said, "but Chato knows this woman. She is Sweetwater the wife of Lobo." Still smiling, he drew his Colt Peacemaker, brought the gun up, pulled back the hammer, spun the chamber and then fired. The Mexican fell to the ground, a bullet through the middle of his head.

The fat One Eye scuttled over, took off the sombrero and scalped him.

"You are hasty, Garcia," Chato

interrupted, as One Eye felt inside the corpse's jacket. "Give me the watch."

Garcia sheepishly threw the watch up to Chato, who caught it. He opened it, wound it up slowly and put it to his ear, his eyes fixed steadily on Sweetwater's face as he listened to its chime.

"It's a funny thing time, uh, Sweetwater," he said. "It comes and goes, and it brought you here." He was unaffected as she turned away.

"Get down," he commanded, but she still sat the horse. He was quickly at her side and his two strong arms pulled her off. She lay in the dust where she had fallen, and Chato kicked dust into her face and hair, a spoiled child in a tantrum.

He grabbed her. She struggled in vain as he dragged her between the two wagons but still out of Lobo's firing-range.

"Lobo," he yelled at the frustrated band of Apaches. "Look what I have, Lobo."

He dragged Sweetwater to her feet with one hand, still waving frantically at them with the other. Lobo sat impassively, peering against the sun at the two figures.

Chato kicked the woman round the legs. "Call his name woman. Let him know I have you."

Sweetwater swivelled her head and spat full into Chato's face.

"Bitch," he screamed as the spittle ran down his cheek. Then he struck her hard across the face. She swayed with the force of the blow but did not go down.

Then Chato's knife was out and the point against her throat. He moved it slowly from throat to chin and then rested the point against her nose.

"Scream when I tell you, Sweetwater, or I cut off your nose and make you ugly."

But still she said nothing, and the anger in Chato boiled over. It was an unbearable force and he began to move the knife into her skin.

"Lobo," Sweetwater's scream rent the air.

Lobo, in the distance, whirled, eyes narrowing as he heard the familiar voice. "Sweetwater," Lobo boomed out the emotional reaction, a charge of anger running under it.

It was just in time to distract the half-breed. Sweetwater's nose was cut and bleeding but not yet distorted as Chato withdrew the knife and looked out across the expanse at Lobo.

"She stays with me, Lobo. She is fair exchange for the Mexican woman, uh, amigo? Stay your distance or you will die with your wife."

Snake Eye's restraining arm held Lobo in check. "We must wait," he urged, "as you so often told us, and attack them when we have an advantage. Do not risk all."

Lobo knew, somewhere deep in the cauldron of his emotions, that Snake Eye's words were wise, but he did not like it. His emotions rebelled against the physical signal he gave to his

Apaches to return to their camp.

Chato smiled as they rode off. Immediately, he chained Sweetwater to one of the wagons. He was pleased with the extra insurance her presence gave him. More than ever now Lobo would think hard before attacking.

"If Lobo makes us run she will be trampled in the dust." Chato laughed, and Garcia the one eye joined him in his mirth.

Chato led the party from the front. Garcia, anxious not to offend again, hung back a little.

"Where do you take us, Chato?" Garcia asked as they rode across a mesa.

"We go back to the stronghold, fool. Lobo has been humiliated as I once was when I had to leave the Apaches to live with scum like you."

The Mexican flushed and hung back again. Though angry, he controlled himself, for he knew that Chato was a wily leader. Even his third-rate intelligence could see that, and also he realised that Chato's knowledge of the territory was second to none and useful when you hunted Apaches for a living. Brutality was all that Garcia knew anyway, and they made a good pair, Chato and he. Beneath the patch was a scarred and sightless eye, the work of an Apache arrow when he was still a boy, and Garcia was determined he would be more cruel to the world than it had ever been to him.

Night was curtaining the sun as they reached the sloping trail which led up from the canyon to the gaping mouth of a huge cave. The wagons were driven inside into the recesses. Chato ordered that the Gatling guns should be taken from them and set at the front of the cave. Then he posted his sentries.

The rest of the men relaxed. They soon lit two fires and sat round in the glow. Somebody started playing an old tune on a harmonica, and feet were tapping. Those inclined started to dance. Chato brought out jugs of whisky and gave them to various groups who took them avidly. A fight broke out, encouraged by enthusiastic whoops and shouts.

Chato left them to it and retreated into the shadows where the wagons stood. He bent over Sweetwater and checked her chains as she sat in the dust.

"It is fitting," he sneered at her, "that my enemy's wife lies in the dust."

The woman cursed him as he returned to the merrymaking. She hoped that Lobo would come for her soon.

5

BRANNIGAN squatted and stared hard at the ground, examining the tracks.

"Some 'paches," he announced. "Tell by the marks on the moccasins. Some whites too with wagons. Big Party."

"How old is the trail?" the boy inquired.

"Bout yesterday. That patch of grass is losing its colour where they walked on it."

"Soldiers using Apache scouts?" the boy posed.

"Nope, too many Apaches."

"Do we follow their trail?"

"Yep."

They mounted again and rode on. It struck Brannigan that they'd been out two days so far and he had no complaint to make about the boy. The youngster hadn't complained about the pace he was setting and he knew how to keep his peace. Brannigan liked that, liked people who didn't run away at the mouth. Besides, he hadn't a lot to say himself for the fury was still in him, a quietly boiling fury deep down, waiting to explode into a blood orgy when he found Lobo the object of it. It had been there a long time and Brannigan knew that the only cure for it now was that either he or Lobo should die. He guessed the boy knew this and that was why he didn't bother him.

"Look!"

Brannigan's thoughts were interrupted by the boy's shout, and he followed his gaze.

A cloud of black smoke was billowing into the blue sky east of them, curling round a butte, the only movement against a motionless backdrop.

"Lobo?" the boy asked. Brannigan squinted against the sun.

"Let's take a look, but real easy."

They rode quickly towards the butte. Brannigan reined in short of it and pointed high into some rocks.

"Let's go over it and come down from above. We might run into a mess of Injuns if we just ride round."

Chato wiped the blood from his knife and nodded to the red-haired gringo and the Mexican who held the scalped lifeless body of the white man. They let him go and he fell to the ground like an empty sackcloth.

He walked over to the burning wagon and thrust his hands close to the flames, throwing back his head and laughing crazily as they licked around his fingers.

Another scalped body lay on the ground near the wagon, and Garcia was untying the gunbelt. He smiled with satisfaction for it was magnificently studded with silver coins, but his smile soon changed to a grimace when he tried to put it on and found that his swollen belly was too big for it. He threw it to the ground in disgust, and one of the men was quick to pick it up.

Garcia stormed over to the two men who held the Apache, drew back his podgy fist and sank it into the Indian's stomach. The Apache doubled up but did not cry out.

"Why don't we kill him now, Garcia?" one of the men asked. "My arms are tired holding him."

"We are saving him, amigo. We will have much fun later." Garcia had been pulling something from his saddle-bag as he spoke, and now he caressed a bullwhip, silver studs embedded along its whole length. He walked back to the Apache and held the handle of the whip under his chin, tilting the head up so that their eyes met.

Then Garcia, grinning, stepped back two yards, uncoiled the whip, raised it slowly and with expert timing brought the tip of the lash down across the Apache's chest. The Apache winced, and Garcia coiled the whip again scowling at the Apache, preparing to give him another dose.

It was fortunate for the Indian that

Ed Brannigan and the boy chose that moment to start their horses sliding down the scree at a sideways angle, sending loose rock ahead of them.

"Riders coming," someone shouted, and the scalp-hunters' hands went automatically to their holsters. Then they relaxed a little when they saw that the two riders were white men. Chato walked over to Garcia.

"What do we do, boss?" one of the men asked as Chato's eyes searched the oncoming riders.

"Get the woman under cover," Chato snapped. "Then we do nothing till we see who these two are. Men tell secrets when they think they are among friends — then whizz." Chato drew his fingers across his throat.

Brannigan rode in first, slow and easy, like he had said, and the boy followed. He had ascertained from the top of the butte that they were white men and he had wanted to ride on but the boy had persuaded him to ride down. A grumbling Brannigan had agreed; but now the uneasiness he felt made him wish he'd sat this one out. He knew when men were looking at him with an over-done curiosity. These men were too wary, but the cards were dealt and he had to play them. They dismounted slowly.

His eyes had already casually taken in the Mexican with the whip, the men holding the Apache, the scalped bodies, and now he brought them into sharper focus. The silence among the scalp-hunters spoke louder than words; it said it was up to him to make the first move.

Chato's confident stance portrayed him as their leader, so Brannigan approached and faced him.

"Thought you was in trouble. Came down to help," he drawled. He nodded at the bodies. "Looks like you took care of it yourself."

Chato's face broke into the almost habitual false smile. "Si, señor, that is right as you see."

"Did these fellers bother you?"

Brannigan gestured at the dead bodies, and the boy saw them now for the first time. Thoughts of Johnson flooded back, and he turned away to be sick. Garcia laughed.

"No! No!" Chato insisted. "These men were killed and scalped by the Apache. We are dealing with one we caught."

Brannigan nodded compliance, but he knew Chato was lying, knew his men were scalp-hunters, but it was a bad time to argue the point.

Garcia came over and walked round Brannigan and the boy. "You carry gold, mister?" he asked, but Chato silenced him with a look.

"How are you called?" Chato asked, turning again.

"My name is Brannigan."

"Brannigan." Chato almost shouted the name, the look on his face dumbfounded. "You are Brannigan?"

"You know me?"

Chato laughed. "You have killed thirty Apache and you ask me this?"

"Ain't you afraid I might kill you and make it thirty and a half?"

Chato's face grew thunderous at Brannigan's words, and the latter wondered if he had gone too far. He knew he had to stand up to Chato, but perhaps he'd overplayed it. He smiled a sickly smile and Chato relaxed.

"A good joke," the half-breed laughed. "Come and have coffee and you can tell me about those thirty. Some may even have been my half-brothers."

The half-breed snapped his fingers at two malingerers leaning against the wagon. They brought blankets and spread them. Meanwhile, the boy wandered over to the two men holding the Apache. At his approach the Indian's head snapped up and the boy instantly recognised the beaten face. It was the young Apache who had attacked him.

Brannigan and Chato sat down, and Garcia, still standing, worked his way to the back of Brannigan and leered down over him.

"There's one thing before we start," Brannigan opened.

"What's that?" Chato asked.

"I don't like people standing behind me. Especially fat greasy Mexicans!" Brannigan spoke the words with contempt, without even turning his head. Chato saw Garcia wince but held up his hand in a restraining signal.

"Go and amuse yourself, Garcia," Chato ordered. The Mexican hesitated, thought momentarily about going for his gun, then shuffled away cursing under his breath. He passed the boy who came over and squatted on the blanket beside Brannigan.

"Now, compadres, where were you going?" Chato spoke in his half-Mexican voice. His eyes moved from Brannigan to the boy.

"We're going after Lobo." For the first time the boy had spoken out of place and was silenced by the look Brannigan gave him. Chato leaned back satisfied.

"There's business for us all then," he

announced, "if you are interested."

Brannigan wasn't interested, but he knew he had no choice. It would be impossible for them to ride away safely from this hard bunch.

"Yup, we're interested," he lied, glaring at the boy.

"I know your reputation, Brannigan," Chato went on. "Why don't we join forces to catch our common enemy?"

"Okay." Brannigan sounded nonchalant. "Long as I get him it don't matter how. But one question."

"What's that?"

"Who gets Lobo if we catch him?"

"I can watch while you kill him," Chato lied this time.

"Suits me."

At that Brannigan got up, went to the horses and started unsaddling them. The boy followed and stood watching him.

"I'm sorry," he said, "for telling 'em we're after Lobo."

"It's done now."

The youngster swallowed, embarrassed. "What are these men?" he asked, looking round at the assorted bunch of hardcases.

"They're scalp-hunters," Brannigan replied. "They take Apache scalps for money. Any age. Any sex. Makes no difference."

The boy recoiled.

"Do the government allow that?" he asked, amazement in his voice.

Brannigan paused. "The Mexican government offers them money. They want the Apaches wiped out. Didn't you know that?"

The boy shook his head. He could not grasp the idea of killing another man for money.

"That's wrong," he said, his voice definite, and Brannigan turned to face him.

"If it was anybody but Apaches," Brannigan said bitterly, "it would be wrong."

The boy went silent and watched Brannigan throw his saddle with the decorative Apache scalps on to the ground. He lay down near his own saddle wondering about Brannigan. Soon the Indian fighter lay down too. The siesta was welcome for both man and boy.

The boy was awakened by a sound he thought was gunfire and sat upright wiping his eyes. Brannigan pushed his hat off his head, opened his eyes briefly, and then pulled the hat down again.

Then the boy saw what had awakened him. Spotted Tail had been tied to one of the wagons and red weals running across his chest told their tale. Garcia stood near the Apache, whip in hand, ready to mete out more punishment. Horror struck the boy again; this was another page in the catalogue of cruelty he had seen perpetrated since he left home. He shook Brannigan who half sat up, saw Garcia with the whip, and turned over again.

"Go to sleep," he mumbled, "it's

only an Apache. They'd do worse to us if they could."

The boy saw that Brannigan was not going to help and took matters into his own hands. He leapt to his feet, took the canteen from his saddle, and strode purposefully to the wagon where Garcia was poised, whip in hand. He brushed past the Mexican, ignoring him and bent over the kneeling Indian.

Garcia watched in amazement, frozen into disbelief, as the boy spilled drops of water from the canteen on to the Apache's parched lips. The Indian licked the water from the corner of his mouth, opened his brown eyes and nodded his head in thanks.

Then the crack of the whip resounded again and a wisp of sand rose from the ground near the boy. He paused, ignored it and went on pouring water into Spotted Tail's mouth. Then came the second angry whiplash and the pain needled across the boy's back bringing tears to his eyes.

“Get out of the way, Gringo,” Garcia shouted frenetically. “Get out of the way or I’ll have your scalp.”

He raised the whip again, and the boy, half turning towards the Mexican, prepared himself for more pain. But, suddenly, Garcia was catapulting through the air, and there was a thud as his heavy carcass hit the ground knocking the wind out of him.

The boy saw Brannigan holding the other end of the whip, standing over Garcia. One of the scalp-hunters made a move for his gun, but before he had cleared the leather Brannigan’s Colt was in his hand pointing accusingly at the offender.

Garcia lay on the ground moaning and holding his back, as Chato, a mean look on his face, stepped down from one of the wagons. He came over to Garcia and Brannigan, quickly assessing what had happened and not liking it. He stood over Garcia watching him squirm as he glowered down at him, and then drove his foot hard into the Mexican's ribs. "Fool," he exploded, so that they all heard and raised his foot again, but Garcia was already crawling away on all fours.

"Back off," Chato snapped at some of the scalp-hunters who had advanced on Brannigan. Then he turned.

"You were foolish, Brannigan. I do not like to see anybody else humiliate my men. It makes me look weak."

"If you kill me," Brannigan said grimly, "you will not find Lobo so easily."

Chato nodded his assent.

"That's why I let you live."

Brannigan holstered his gun. All present recognised this as a preliminary round. The inevitable finale would come later.

The boy used his bandana to wipe the sweat from Spotted Tail's brow. The Apache's eyes darted to and fro like a baited animal's, but throughout his ordeal he had never cried out. All his training went against the admission of pain. When he had settled, the expression in his eyes showed appreciation of the boy's help.

"Thanks," the boy said when he finally settled back down beside Brannigan.

The latter raised himself on to his elbows. "That was a foolish thing you done," he barked. Then softer, "But brave too."

"Why did you help me?" The boy was intense.

Brannigan yawned. "Let's just say I've taken an instant dislike to that greaser." He indicated Garcia who was leaning sulkily against a wagon.

"We'll have to watch him," the boy said. "He'll really hate you now."

Brannigan grunted a reply, and the conversation ended. Jim tried to resist sleep but felt the need of it and was soon away. He did not come to until late afternoon, when Brannigan shook him awake and handed him a mug of coffee.

"They're staying here tonight," he

whispered, "and moving out in the morning."

"We really staying then?"

"They'll be watching us," Brannigan replied, "but if the chance comes — " His voice tailed away.

6

NEXT day they rode hard, Chato driving them on. He wanted to return quickly to the camp and refurbish their supplies. Brannigan's presence was a spur in his side. Lobo could not evade them both for ever.

As they rode through the canyon to the cave Brannigan memorised its geography, imprinting every feature on his brain, figuring it might be useful knowledge if they had to escape.

When Chato fired a warning shot a sentry appeared on a needle rock above them. Brannigan figured the sentry had a good position and if he was a good shot could pick off anybody entering or leaving, especially since the entrance to the valley was narrow, but then suddenly widened giving him a fair chance of shooting down riders as they came through.

The track up to the cave was narrow, and Brannigan observed the barricade of rocks at the entrance — a good place to defend.

When the wagons were inside the cave he and the boy watched the scalp-hunters busy themselves stocking them with fresh food and ammunition while Garcia hovered over them. The proceedings were slow, for these men, as Brannigan wryly observed, were not used to this kind of work. They lived easy, and the money they got from their bounties was spent mainly on booze. The boy heard one red-headed scalp-hunter curse them as lazy bastards as he staggered past with an ammunition box.

Spotted Tail was still tied to the wagon, and at intervals the boy gave him water. Nobody interfered with him this time, though Garcia watched venomously. Brannigan couldn't work it out; couldn't figure why anybody would want to help an Apache.

The Indian fighter passed the time cleaning and polishing his Colt and checking his gunbelt. Once, when Garcia looked over, he held up a bullet and twisted it in his fingers so that the sunlight caught it and it sparkled. Then he pointed to Garcia who understood the gesture and sullenly turned away.

Brannigan, it was, who spotted the woman before any of them. She appeared out of the cave and started to edge her way down the track, pressing her body hard against the rock. Brannigan nudged the boy and together they watched her progress.

She was five yards in the clear when she started to run, but, simultaneously, one of the scalp-hunters, a great brute of a man, lumbered into the light and saw her. It only took seconds for him to catch her and engulf her in a massive pair of arms and lift her up.

Chato, hearing sounds of a scuffle, turned from the conversation he was having with one of his men and saw what had happened. Instantly he strode over to the man and woman. It was obvious from his wild gestures that he was angry, and the man looked sheepish. Brannigan saw Chato gesture to the boy and himself and figured Chato had not wanted them to see the incident. Then he noticed Spotted Tail. He was straining and jerking at his bonds, his eyes on the woman, never wavering; he obviously knew her.

"Did you see Spotted Tail?" the boy asked.

"Yeah, I saw."

"He knew the Apache woman, didn't he? Who do you think she is?"

"Couldn't guess. Mebbe his woman, but he's a bit young to be wed."

The boy considered. "Maybe I could ask him."

"Think he'd tell you?" Brannigan was cynical again.

"I could try anyway."

Brannigan shrugged. "Please yourself, but I wouldn't believe a word he said."

Then Chato was walking over to

them. "You saw that little fracas, uh?" he inquired, standing a yard from them. "Women, uh! They always cause trouble." His eyes were searching their faces for reaction, but he saw none, and neither replied. "That one, uh — " he said gesturing to the mouth of the cave — "that one is the wife of one of my men. She's always trying to get away from him. Last winter when we were freezing he threatened to eat her." The half-breed was roaring with laughter.

Then he turned away, evidently assured that they had drawn no conclusions from the incident.

"That settles it," Brannigan said when he was well out of earshot. "Chato was real anxious to explain her away. He wouldn't have bothered if she was just a squaw." He was stroking his chin, deep in thought.

"Would they really eat a squaw?" the boy asked, looking round at the scalp-hunters.

Brannigan laughed, a rare event for him.

"Heard of it once or twice when trappers have been wintering and run out of food."

The boy turned pale and decided to change the subject.

"I'll ask the Apache about the woman. Maybe she is a hostage or something. Will he speak English?"

"Some do, some don't," Brannigan said noncommittally, showing no interest, which annoyed the boy. Seconds later he was walking over to the wagons, stung again into action by Brannigan's indifference.

As the boy's shadow fell across him, Spotted Tail looked up, eyes burning in their sockets. They blazed defiance which settled into a gentler resignation when they made out his recent benefactor. The water which the boy poured on to his parched lips revived him and he was grateful to the White Eyes, the first ever to help him. He acknowledged it with a proud nod of the head. Then Jim leant closer.

"Who is she? You know her, don't you?"

But the Indian was stubbornly silent, and the boy poured more water on to his lips.

"We are not with these cruel men," he went on. "Maybe we need each other." The boy watched the flicker of indecision in the Apache's eyes gradually resolve itself.

"She is Sweetwater, wife of Lobo." The voice was hoarse when it came, but the meaning unmistakable, and the boy knew instantly why the Apache had tried to escape his bonds.

"Don't worry," he whispered, "there is still hope."

"What'd he tell you?" For once Brannigan was inquisitive.

"That woman is Lobo's wife," the boy stated blandly. He saw Brannigan fight down the excitement rising in him so that when he spoke his voice was level.

"That's it then. When we go, we take her with us, then Lobo will either come for us or let us get to him."

"Do you have to use the woman?"

"I'd use anything, boy, anything to get near Lobo."

"What about the Apache?"

"What about him?"

The boy drew in his breath, sucked it into his cheeks and let it go.

"You can't leave him."

Brannigan's eyebrows knitted together in a frown. "There you go," he said. "Can't you get it into your head they're killers? They killed my wife, the sons of bitches."

"What are you then?" the boy asked sharply.

The boy instantly regretted his words. He saw Brannigan colour and sweep back his arm to strike, but in the nick of time he checked himself and lowered it slowly.

"When I decide it's time to go you be ready," Brannigan said, breaking the edgy silence.

"I don't like leaving him," the boy said ruefully.

Then they were silent, both angry for their own reasons. The boy hadn't wanted to quarrel, but he didn't see how taking one more with them would make such a difference, even though he was Apache. He would never let any man be tortured if he could help it. The spectre of Johnson haunted his young brain.

For the rest of that day Brannigan and the boy hardly spoke. It was when the night was at its darkest, a blanket to their conspiracy, that Brannigan shook the boy awake and pushed some strips of rawhide into his hands. Brannigan's voice rapped out orders.

"Get to the corral, boy, hobble their horses and make it tight. I'll try for the woman."

"Can you find her?"

"You do your job and I'll do mine. Separate off three horses and I'll get to you."

"Four horses, ain't it?" The boy's voice was pleading. He had not forgotten Spotted Tail.

Brannigan nodded a gruff compliance. "He's your responsibility then. There's a guard near the remuda. You leave him to me."

They bellied their way in the dust towards the makeshift remuda which confined the horses. They could hear the disharmonious orchestra of snoring from the bedded scalp-hunters. The boy thought of a dangerous jungle full of strange animal noises.

When the quarter moon sank further behind a cloud Brannigan raised himself slightly. The boy imitated him, but only to find his face thrust into the dust again. Out of one eye, he sneaked a look sideways at Brannigan and saw that his head too was close to the earth. Turning, but still low, he saw the reason — the red glow of a cigarette end betrayed the presence of a sentry in a position ahead, adjacent to the remuda. Brannigan raised himself again.

"When you see the cigarette go out," he whispered, drawing his knife from its sheath, "start crawling for the horses."

The boy watched Brannigan disappear into the darkness, and then the red glow ahead held his eyes like a magnet.

It seemed an age before he saw a red spark shoot in a curve through the blackness and then die; he knew it was time to crawl.

When he reached the remuda he crawled in through the horses' legs and began hobbling. Then, suddenly, a strange warm sensation crept up his back and he wondered if the demented Garcia was standing over him playing some kind of evil trick. He whipped round on to his back and let out a sigh of relief. One of the horses had just finished urinating over him. Uncomfortably, he went on with his task; it could have been worse. When he had finished he cut out four horses and waited for Brannigan.

Meanwhile the Indian fighter had sneaked into the cave. The camp fires were dying as he crept deeper inside, beneath the flickering shadows on the cave wall.

His keen eyes straining, he searched the gloom, but there was no sign of any human. But, in the deepest part of the cave, he felt his foot hit something hard and, looking down, saw that it was a large stone slab projecting from the flat floor. A faint flicker of yellow light at one side of the slab betrayed the entrance to a cave below and this was the incentive he needed. His muscles straining to the utmost, he moved the slab to one side.

He saw her below, her frightened face illuminated and ghostly in the light of the single candle as she looked up at the intruder. Brannigan, acting quickly, dropped down the hole and stood beside her, a towering, imposing figure next to her diminutive form. She nodded her head occasionally as he explained in Apache that he was going to get her out. Then he made a leap for the edge of the hole, gripped it and hauled himself out. Sweetwater took the hand he offered her, and with a struggle he pulled her up and out into the large cave.

They moved along the wall. As they were approaching the entrance, Brannigan motioned for her to slow up as they neared the sleeping scalp-hunters.

They were near the wagon to which Spotted Tail was tied when Brannigan remembered his promise. The woman remained in the shadows as Brannigan cut the Apache's bonds, muttering a few words in explanation. The Indian was weak, and Brannigan had to help him back to the woman, but he was glad, for a fit Apache could have been an awkward customer.

When they were almost safely out of the cave the giant shadow loomed against the cave wall and Brannigan felt the chill fear which primitive man must have felt when threatened by the unknown. He whirled on his heel, pushing the two Indians to one side. Then the full force of Chato's body hit him as he grabbed for his knife.

The wind went out of him, but as he fell, the instinct of the frontiersman hammered home the message — hold on to your knife. He sensed Chato prepare to launch himself again and rolled quickly, but leaving his knife, gripped in an immovable fist, blade upwards. An agonised scream rent the air as Chato landed, the knife tearing into his thigh muscle; the warm, sticky feeling Brannigan experienced oozing over his knife-hand was Chato's blood.

Then he pulled the knife out as Chato rolled in agony. Hastily he ushered the two Apaches out of the cave.

As they crossed the front of the cave the scalp-hunters were stirring, disturbed by Chato's screams. Fortunately, the darkness was causing confusion as he pushed the Apaches towards the remuda. He hoped that the boy had done his job.

He was relieved to see Jim standing there, anxiously holding the four horses. In silence he helped Brannigan get

Sweetwater and Spotted Tail mounted, and then the two whites climbed up as the shouts of the scalp-hunters, panicking in the darkness, reached a harsh crescendo.

"Yipee. Let's go," Brannigan screamed into the night, and the four horses accelerated into a gallop. One of the scalp-hunters, a dark silhouette, leapt at Brannigan's horse, but its rider's leg shot out and caught him full in the mouth. Sweetwater rode another offender down with her horse. A few loose shots followed them as they hit the trail down from the cave and disappeared into the blackness.

Chaos reigned behind them. The scalp-hunters made straight for the horses and tried to mount, but the boy had done his work well. The hobbled horses started to buck, frustrating the attempts to mount them.

As the four fugitives sped through the entrance to the stronghold they heard the loud crack of the sentry's rifle, but he was shooting blind. Brannigan did not even bother to return the fire.

They rode on into the night, and it was several miles before Brannigan called a halt. The panting horses stood motionless as he studied the back trail. Spotted Tail he considered to be too weak to try anything, while Sweetwater was sitting silently astride her bronco. Dismounting, he lay on his belly and, ear to the ground, listened for sounds of pursuit. There were none.

"Lost 'em," he stated, looking up, "but they'll be coming."

"Where to now?" the boy asked.

Brannigan stroked his chin. "That's up to the woman. She knows where Lobo'll be. We'll make for high ground. See the night out there."

So they rode on, following Brannigan who felt keen-edged anticipation riding with him. The woman could be the answer, the last link in his quest.

7

THEY made high ground easily enough, and Brannigan searched for a good place where he could assess the situation and question the woman.

Spotted Tail had managed somehow, in his weakened condition, to stay the pace, whilst the boy was wondering at the complications which had now arisen. When he had set out, it had simply been an individual matter; he wanted his horse back. Now there were others involved and he was beginning to care what the outcome would be for them, especially Brannigan.

He remembered his mother telling him that nothing was ever pure black or pure white, and now he thought he knew what she meant. He liked Brannigan, but he could see the dark, evil side to him and it frightened him.

It was the same with the Apaches. He sensed a certain self-assurance in them which he respected, but alongside that there was always the savage, the twist in nature which had been responsible for Johnson's horrific death. But he had no doubts about the scalp-hunters; they were worse than any Apache. He figured that the Apaches had to be violent to survive, but the scalp-hunters had chosen to trade in the traffic of human lives and that could never be right.

They reined in amongst some high boulders. When they had dismounted Brannigan ordered the boy to stand guard and, turning to the woman, indicated for her to get down. Then they, in turn, helped the still weak Spotted Tail. When they were all settled Brannigan motioned the woman over to him and stared straight into her eyes.

"I want Lobo. I'm going to kill him," he stated plainly.

She returned his hard look and then dragged her eyes away and stared vacantly into space.

"I know this," she said. "I have heard of Brannigan."

"I'll do a trade," Brannigan went on. "If you will take me to Lobo, I will give you back when he agrees to settle the business between us." He spoke in a flat, low tone, but the woman registered no surprise.

"I will not take you. I would betray my husband." She said nothing more, but studied Brannigan who picked up some loose sand and let it run through his fingers. Finally he shrugged.

"It makes no difference. In the end I'll still find him and kill him."

"Or he will kill you."

"Possible." Brannigan paused. "Anyhow, he'll come for me now. He will know I have you."

"Yes, but the difference is that I will not betray him," Sweetwater replied.

"Then we have nothing else to say." Brannigan started into the saddle as he spoke, and the woman helped the silent Spotted Tail up.

When the boy joined them they rode out, still on the high ground, and Brannigan still not knowing where he was going, except that he was putting distance between the scalp-hunters and themselves. He did not brood over the woman's refusal, for he knew that Lobo would, in the end, find them. Lobo would come, and when he did, possession of the woman would give him an ace in the pack.

In fact, Lobo had already received news of a small party of riders, one of them an Apache woman who looked like his wife. Now he was leading a party of warriors after them.

Meanwhile, after some miles, the sound of voices, white men's voices, brought Brannigan's group to an abrupt halt. The Indian fighter motioned for the boy to ease back, and made signs for the two Apaches to dismount. When they were down he dismounted himself and ordered the boy to watch the Indians and handed him his own Colt.

"I'll take a look ahead," he whispered, shouldering his Henry, his eyes on the rock ahead where the voices had come from. He scuttled off and seconds later was viewing the source of the disturbance. The uniforms of three soldiers stood out, vivid blue against the grey rock and pale sand. Brannigan instantly recognised the sergeant as O'Leary, a reputed bully back at the fort. The others were unknown to him.

O'Leary was heating water in a billy-can over the fire round which they were all squatting, talking loudly. But there was a fourth figure, an Indian who was staked out, and it was on him that Brannigan concentrated his attention. The size of his body told Brannigan that he was no more than ten years old. Why did they want one so young? The only purpose, he reasoned, was to collect the money for the scalp, and he felt sick at the thought; pity, an emotion that he had not felt for a long time, welled up inside him. The small figure struggling against the tautness of the rawhide, yet in a controlled way which lent a certain dignity to his efforts, moved Brannigan.

His decision was made quickly. Arriving back at the horses, he took his Spencer from its scabbard explaining to the boy what he had seen.

"I'll pick 'em off easy," he said.

"Thought you wouldn't help no Injun," the boy mumbled, mocking him, but secretly pleased.

"This is different." Brannigan's voice was emphatic. "That kid had no chance. I've never killed an Apache by torture and I figure that's what they intend." Then he was off again.

As he adjusted his sights, one of the soldiers was leaning over the boy, obscuring him from Brannigan's vision. Brannigan levelled the Spencer, waiting for him to turn. From his position, it looked as though the soldier's arms were busy, and it seemed just possible that he was untying the Apache. Then, however, he rose slowly and turned round. Brannigan saw his hands, the black hair hanging loose from them and the red blood dripping, and in his head thunder exploded. Leaping to his feet, he stretched to his full height and let out a full-bellied Apache war cry. The rifle leapt to his shoulder and he was squeezing the trigger. Three shots rang out, chasing each other. The soldier with the scalp got it between the eyes. The other two bullets found identical targets in the back of the neck and, the two by the fire slumped forward. In the immediate stillness which followed, Brannigan could only hear his own breathing. The three bodies below lay like discarded toys.

He stood there, letting the adrenalin settle, whilst the fire below flickered fitfully, protesting its life amongst the dead.

He was still standing there, cradling his rifle, when the others came up. Spotted Tail and Sweetwater fell to their knees next to the body of the boy Apache. Sweetwater's voice wailed out in a death chant as Spotted Tail, eyes working across the scene, pieced together what had happened. When he looked up at Brannigan there was respect in his eyes for his enemy.

The boy was still surveying the carnage before him, when Brannigan came down. Neither spoke, and both knew that this time the violence was justified.

Wordlessly, Brannigan hauled Sweetwater to her feet and pulled her over to the horses. Spotted Tail followed, and Brannigan noted that he appeared to be stronger now; he would have to watch him more closely.

The four rode out away from the death spot. Each one understood rough justice. Spotted Tail and Sweetwater were especially appreciative.

When they were out of sight, the Apache warrior who had watched them go rode into the clearing and scalped the three lifeless soldiers. Picking up the body of the dead Apache boy, he walked back to his waiting horse.

Darkness was approaching when he found Lobo and laid the small body at the chief's feet telling of the vengeance Brannigan had taken.

Lobo listened. He had always known that Brannigan was an exceptional, fearless warrior, but now he felt that he knew another side of him; he was an honourable man. Lobo knew many Apaches who were child-killers and he had no respect for them. Brannigan was white and yet of the same mind as himself in these matters; a man worthy of respect. When warriors met, it should be on equal terms with an equal chance of death and victory. Yes, you could sneak up on a man and kill him. That was fair, the law of the wilderness. You could torture a man, because he knew what he was doing when he rode into the wilderness. But child-killing was different, for a child was an unformed being, to be protected. Anger grew in Lobo when he saw the scalp, a hundred dollar's worth of blood money.

Brannigan was still fuming inside long after the incident. That was probably why he did not notice the rattler. As his horse placed its foot the snake's round head darted out and its fangs sank into the hard flesh of its forefoot. The horse instantly reacted, rising on to its back legs and kicking out as it whinnied its pain and fear. Brannigan fought hard to stay on, clinging with his knees and tightening his grip on the reins. But the horse's panic was too great.

Sweetwater saw her opportunity, weighed up the odds as she scanned the countryside around and kicked the belly of her horse. It shot off towards the low ground which opened into the plain, plunging down the steep, narrow side-trail.

One of Brannigan's hands went for the gun. It made the holster, and he pulled out the Colt but, as he pointed it in the direction of the departing figure, the bucking, kicking horse made the action senseless.

"Get your gun on that 'pache," Brannigan yelled to the boy, who came out of his dream and, after a stuttered draw, covered Spotted Tail. The Apache inwardly cursed his slow wits; the opportunity had gone. Perhaps the boy would not shoot, but he could not be certain.

Brannigan was still fighting his horse when, through the blur of dust, he saw the rattler. Next time the horse came round he pointed the Colt sharply and pulled the trigger, his shot taking the rattler's head off.

At last the horse settled and stood timidly, allowing Brannigan to dismount. He tore open the saddle-bags, took out some rope and threw it at the boy.

"Tie his legs," he snapped, unable to hide his anger, and the boy ordered Spotted Tail down. He did as commanded. Brannigan removed his hat, wiped his brow and swore as he watched the diminishing figure of Sweetwater galloping across the plain.

"We've seen the last of her," the

boy sighed, but Brannigan was already kneeling, examining the horse's leg.

"What are you going to do?" the boy asked as Brannigan looked up.

"I'll need your help. Hold his head and talk to him while I cut the swelling and drain it."

They proceeded with the task. The horse behaved itself, and when he was finished Brannigan tied his bandana round his incision.

"What's left for us now?" the boy asked despondently as Brannigan rose. "Looks like I'll never git my horse back."

Brannigan studied Spotted Tail. "We'll let him go. He's no real good to us anyhow. Wouldn't stop Lobo. I can use his horse and we'll head after the woman. She's still the prize if we can get her 'fore Lobo does."

Brannigan rapped out some words in Apache and Spotted Tail rose from his squatting position. They watched him walk away in the direction from which they had come before Brannigan unloaded the canteens from his own lame horse. "Never mind, fella," he said, stroking the horse's head, "we leave you here. You've still got a chance." When he had finished they rode out.

They rode for an hour in Sweetwater's tracks until Brannigan brought them to a halt, pointing at the dust-cloud ahead. "Looks like Lobo beat us to her," the boy uttered through dry lips.

"Better make sure." Brannigan's reply was bitter with disappointment. "We'll go real cautious and take a looksee."

They headed in the direction of the dust-cloud, and Brannigan soon knew from examining the tracks that it was not Apaches they were pursuing. Unlike the Indian horses, these were shod, and the small star on most of the shoes told him they were the work of the smithy back at the fort; it was his personal trademark. It could be that the cavalry had taken Sweetwater.

"Two riders, sir," the sentry bellowed

across the encircled wagons. "One of 'em looks like Brannigan."

The captain's back straightened as he shouted, "You sure, corporal?"

"Near as certain, sir," the voice boomed again.

Captain Jackson stepped away from the Apache woman to the position outside the wagons occupied by the corporal and stared out into the wilderness, protecting his eyes from the sun with his hat. It crossed his mind that it could be these two from whom the woman had been running.

Brannigan knew that their approach was being watched, and he knew, too, that a lone Apache was following their back trail.

"Are we going right on in?" the boy asked, watching Brannigan inquisitively. "It seems a foolish thing after what happened back there."

Brannigan turned in the saddle and looked back. "There's Apache behind and soldiers ahead. Take your pick."

Both knew which of the choices they preferred and kept heading towards the wagons.

The soldiers let them go right in. As they rode towards the picket-line, Brannigan felt the hairs on his neck prickle. The boy saw the cynical, unsmiling faces of the troopers and felt uneasy.

They dismounted at the picket-line and tied their horses. Captain Jackson strutted over and stood, ramrod straight, a yard away from Brannigan. The boy immediately recognised him as the captain who had displeased him when he had first searched for Brannigan in the fort, with no satisfaction at all. The premonitions of danger he felt now were well founded.

When Captain Jackson's features broke into a smile, Brannigan momentarily was relieved and figured his instinct had been wrong. Then the smile vanished, to be replaced by a mask of hate as he loosened the button on his holster. The Peacemaker came out awkwardly, but Brannigan made no move for his own gun.

"At last we have you, all tied up and legal." Jackson could not hide the satisfaction in his voice, nor did he wish to.

Brannigan stood, waiting, head insolently cocked to one side.

"One of my scouts rode up and found that bloody scene." Jackson's voice rose in oratory. "Three of the best of my men are lying dead back there."

"He didn't do nothing. Those soldiers were — " The boy reeled as the back of the captain's free hand struck him.

"Shut up," Jackson yelled, his small eyes wild and staring. "I told you about him but you wouldn't listen." He was walking round Brannigan who didn't move a muscle. "Three good men," he muttered again, moving over to the camp fire. Brannigan and the boy exchanged wary glances.

Jackson knelt by the fire, drew the knife he carried in his belt and held it in the flames, his face malicious. When he had finished he rose and ordered two troopers to hold Brannigan.

"The army has its own justice out here," he rasped, standing before Brannigan and nodding knowingly at the watching soldiers.

The boy winced as he saw the blade edge towards Brannigan's cheek, but when he made a move forward a pair of powerful arms gripped him from behind.

Brannigan screamed once, short and loud, as the captain precisely carved the small 'T' for traitor on his cheek, and then he slumped forward in a faint.

His sadism satisfied, the captain opened his tunic pocket and took something out. The boy saw him open the locket and throw it down into the dust beside Brannigan. "You made another mistake, feller," he said. "You left a picture of your wife behind."

When Brannigan came round he found the boy cradling his head on his lap. "Hurts like hell," he groaned, feeling his cheek and noting the soldier with the rifle who stood guarding them. He picked up the locket and frowned at his wife's picture.

"We've got to get you out of here," the boy whispered, but Brannigan was still occupied with the picture. He showed it to the boy. It was a picture of a dark-haired girl with lively eyes and a flashing smile. The words 'Elizabeth Brannigan killed by the renegade Lobo' were written across the bottom, obscuring part of the picture.

"She was pretty," the boy stated, surmising that Brannigan expected him to say something and glad of the distraction from the ugly mark on Brannigan's cheek.

"How do you know it was Lobo?" he found himself saying.

"No doubt." Brannigan was emphatic. "The arrows were Mescalero, and on the cabin wall the word 'Lobo' was scratched in blood just like he wanted me to know it was him, the evil devil."

The boy nodded assent and watched Brannigan lie back and shut his eyes. In silent agreement, the boy did likewise. Sleep rode over their tired bodies.

Brannigan awoke as the sun rose, his burned cheek still nagging painfully. He tried not to think of it. A fresh guard, sitting cross-legged five yards away, wore a bored expression.

Brannigan saw that the woman had been brought over and dumped next to them. She was still asleep.

He looked upwards at the silhouette of the Dragoons and the bright light from the morning sun rising behind them. He wondered why the spot was so ill chosen, as he noted the spur of one of the foothills rising above them, a perfect place for an Apache attack.

The red orb slowly topped the highest of the Dragoons and burst into its full glory. Brannigan, however, had no time to admire it, before the familiar high-pitched screaming whistle triggered his warning system. He saw the sentry recoil and fall backwards as the Apache war arrow buried itself in his neck. The expression on his face was not now one of boredom.

Brannigan kicked the boy awake as the air was filled with more ominous wailings, and the first of the soldiers woke to give the alarm. "Free me," Brannigan yelled, offering the boy his bound hands. The latter worked frantically at the knots, eyes wide like a frightened rabbit, as more arrows fell like rain into the camp. Then he saw the knife in the dead soldier's boot and retrieved it.

As the boy cut him free Brannigan saw Jackson on his feet in the middle of the camp, urging his men to the horses. He saw, too, the Apache arrow drive into the captain's stomach and the blood staining his tunic as he dropped slowly to his knees, staring disbelievingly up into the foothills.

Brannigan grabbed the woman, and, taking the knife from the boy, cut her bonds. He half pulled, half dragged her under the nearest wagon, the boy diving after them.

"Lucky as hell she was lying near us," Brannigan said breathlessly, watching the soldiers being slaughtered by the continuous hail of arrows, some of them before they even got out of their blankets. He saw that the picket-line was not far away.

"We might make the horses if we take her. They won't risk hitting her," Brannigan guessed. "You ready?"

The boy nodded, still dazed by the suddenness of the onslaught, and they pushed the woman out in front of them. She tried to run, but Brannigan grabbed her and held her close. The boy kept close to Brannigan as they hurried across to the picket-line. They mounted quickly, Brannigan riding double with the woman, and rode like the wind, away from the slaughter.

Lobo, up on the spur, watched them ride clear. When the last soldier lay dead, he ordered his Apaches to mount and return to their camp. Alone, on the big white, he set off to trail Brannigan.

8

LOBO trailed them all that day. Brannigan was clever, and several times his tricks fooled the Apache, but still Lobo came on and on, relishing the prospect of their meeting. He had not seen his wife for over a year now, and he was keen to have her back with him. As he rode, he planned his strategy, what he would say to the white man when he caught up and how he would bargain. The fact that it was Brannigan who had whittled away at his tribe, and now held his wife captive, was a double-edged incentive.

Meanwhile, ahead, Brannigan did not give much for the chances of the small party. Since they were hunted by the Apaches and scalp-hunters, it meant that there were not many safe places in the territory. As well as that, they were all tired.

They rested, high up in some rocks, and Brannigan watched behind. He unpacked the Henry which he had grabbed back in the soldiers' camp, and leaning it against a rock, unhooked a canteen from one of the saddles and took a swig. The cool, refreshing liquid gurgled in his throat. Satisfied, he passed the canteen to the boy who took a swig and passed it on to the reclining Sweetwater. She drank it greedily until she was satiated.

"What now?" the boy asked.

"We wait."

"For what — death?" The boy's tone betrayed his impatience.

Brannigan turned from his vigil. "We've nowhere to go," he said, sounding a little pleased at the thought. Perhaps he wanted to be cornered by Lobo.

"Nowhere's safe, but — " he hesitated, turning back to the trail — "I won't think anything less of you if you get out and try to make it back to the fort. After all, boy, you only came for a darned horse."

"No thanks!" The boy was indignant. "I've come this far and I intend to get my horse."

Brannigan grinned. "Mebbe I'll bury you with the horse."

The boy looked back at him, returning the smile. "Mebbe I'll bury you with Lobo."

They focused their concentration on the trail once more. Brannigan narrowed his eyes until they were slits and wiped the perspiration from his brow. He pointed to the horizon, and the boy saw the small dot coming into view. They watched it gradually growing larger, a slow, mesmerising emergence into human form.

As he came into rifle range, the Apache halted and sat motionless on the horse. The boy's eyes ached with straining. Brannigan levelled the Henry. "Come on, you tricky son of a bitch," he muttered in the ominous silence, but the figure stood still.

The boy, senses awakened by the new

danger, kept a wary eye on Sweetwater. She, however, was still reclining, eyes fixed straight ahead.

Lobo had judged his distance to perfection. He knew they were up there, and his long experience had lent him expertise when it came to staying just out of range.

"Sweetwater!" The echo of Lobo's voice bounced off the rocks around Brannigan and the boy.

Brannigan nodded to the woman. "Show him you have heard," he snapped at her, a greedy anticipation in his tone which he could not hide.

She stood up slowly and stood out from behind the rocks. Lobo, seeing her, quickly cupped his hands round his mouth again.

"If he wishes to come, bring him my woman," he yelled. "Your husband commands this. Lobo does not fear Brannigan."

Brannigan smiled, a smile like that of a man who is approaching delirium, a frightening smile to the boy. He looked at the woman who wore a pained expression.

"We will come, tell him." His voice was eager again.

The woman cupped her hands. "He comes. Brannigan comes to die," she shouted.

They watched Lobo turn the white and ride slowly away towards the horizon, an ever-diminishing figure. Nobody spoke. The boy felt he was watching death itself come and go. But always, burned on his memory, was the sight of the Apache chief riding down the hill to free him from the Lypan. The strange contradiction confused him and ate away at his clear-cut views of good and evil men.

They rode out later, when Lobo had disappeared, following in his wake, the relentless sun still burning down on them. Brannigan had tied a rope round the woman's waist and the other end was round his middle so that a distance of never less than six feet was between them. He wasn't about to lose his high card so near to winning the pot.

Lobo's trail was clear most of the way. When it became indistinct, Sweetwater urged herself out in front, complying with her husband's wishes and keeping them on the trail to the camp. It seemed to the boy, as the day wore on, that she was speeding up, urging the pace. She led them along trails that even Brannigan did not know existed, twisting and turning her horse through the canyon-riddled Dragoons.

As the evening approached, Brannigan sensed, with all the sureness of his frontier experience, that the Apaches were watching them, the encroaching gloom an unnecessary yet helpful accomplice to their hidden presence. He chose their camping place carefully, the nearness of his enemies in mind. That night Sweetwater lay close to him, the barrel of the Henry pressed close against her temple as a warning to those unseen presences. But Brannigan did not sleep; his whole body was attuning itself to what lay ahead, and he could feel the rapid drumming of the blood in his veins. The boy, too exhausted to resist, slept well, as, with all the practical sense of an Apache, did Sweetwater.

The next day it did not take long for the two Mescalero warriors to appear on their trail about fifty yards back. The boy felt uneasy, but Brannigan, chin set, rode stubbornly on lending the boy some courage. The set of his head, the immobile features, coupled with the rhythmical pace of the horse reminded that boy of a funeral procession, Brannigan, the chief pall-bearer, ashen grey with trail dust. Memories of his father's funeral drifted back and nostalgia swept over him as he remembered his father's gentleness and the good life he had promised his wife and son. Nostalgia soon gave way to resolution; he would at least fulfil his father's dreams for his mother's sake, and the big white was vital for that task.

Occasionally, the boy glanced back at

the two Apaches. They were still there, preserving the same distance between the whites and themselves, fifty yards, no more, no less. At times they would disappear behind rocks, but only to re-emerge and follow.

Once, when the boy looked back, Brannigan said, without turning, "They're shutting the gates, boy. No going back now."

In the late afternoon other mounted Mescaleros appeared, one by one, on their flanks. Brannigan stopped, untied the rope again round his waist and pulled Sweetwater closer. Then he tied the rope again, the distance between them reduced to a yard. The Henry was still pressed against the woman's temple, while he held the reins with his other hand.

When the first, unmounted Apache appeared out of nowhere, the boy winced in surprise. Brannigan felt the sweat on the palms of his hands making the rifle-stock slippery. He tightened his grip as other braves appeared.

One Apache took an arrow from his quiver and fitted it to his bow. The hairs on the back of the boy's neck prickled. As they rode past, the Indian pointed the bow in their direction, tracing their movement with the tip of the arrow. They were close enough to see his rotting, black teeth as he snarled at them. Brannigan leant over the boy's horse and spat. The spittle hit the Apache flush on the cheek. His snarling mouth showed more of his black teeth, but, to the boy's relief, he did not release the arrow.

Then other bows were levelled at them. Brown fingers held the tension-wrought gut, and the boy hoped that nobody would slip up.

"Don't worry," Brannigan said out of the side of his mouth. "If Lobo had ordered it, we would have been dead hombres miles back. They daren't go against him. All this is just show."

The wickiups appeared ahead, nestled in a rocky valley. Some women sat outside grinding maize and children ran around playing. For the boy it was a surprising scene of domesticity, in contrast to the wild faces of the braves around him.

They proceeded through the throng of angry men, Brannigan scouring the camp with his eyes, looking for Lobo.

Suddenly he was there, ahead and to the left. The Indians fell away before them, forming a corridor of bodies leading to their chief who sat astride the big white. The boy studied the chief's features as they approached: the long nose and flared nostrils, the large generous mouth and the high forehead. A red headband restricted the flowing hair, and his big chest bulged beneath the black shirt he wore. He leant forward, hands on the big white's neck, watching them approach.

They pulled up three yards away. Some of the Apaches closed in, but, at a signal from Lobo, retreated again. Brannigan and Lobo stared hard at each other, and then, as they moved on to the woman, the Apache's brown eyes softened perceptibly.

Brannigan, still staring fixedly at Lobo, bit his bottom lip to stem his excitement.

"You see how it is." Brannigan spoke first, hate and arrogance in his tone.

"I see. What is it you want?"

"You."

Lobo shrugged nonchalantly. "Every white man wants Lobo, but with you, Brannigan, with you it is different. The hate lives in you. I see it in your face and hear it in your voice. When you kill my braves I feel it here." Lobo pointed to his heart. "Why is this, white man?"

Brannigan pointed wordlessly at Sweetwater. "How do you like it, Lobo? Your woman like this, uh?" There was venom in his voice, and Lobo's eyes flickered on to the finger edging the trigger of the Henry.

"You fight women, Brannigan? The warrior who killed soldiers to avenge an Apache boy will also kill an Apache woman?"

Brannigan leant his head back and

laughed ironically.

"You kill my wife then reproach me about killing women. That's rich. Apaches kill women all over the southwest."

Lobo's nostrils flared at Brannigan's words, insulting in front of his braves.

"I lived some time up at the mission in Sonora," he said proudly. "I learned the evil of killing women. None of my Mescaleros kill women, and I did not kill your wife."

Brannigan laughed, ironically again, a touch of hysteria in the sound which made the boy uneasy.

"No more talk, Lobo. A year back, near Sonora, you killed and scalped my wife, and now you have to pay."

"We have not been to Sonora for two years."

Brannigan sighed theatrically so that Lobo heard. "No more lies, Lobo, no more talk," he said. "Ride south to Table Butte. I will be there with the woman. Come alone and we will fight. Then the woman is free."

Lobo nodded his agreement as the boy tugged at Brannigan's sleeve. "What about my horse?" he whispered. The Indian fighter turned back to the chief.

"Bring the big white too, Lobo. That's part of the trade."

Lobo nodded again. They backed off and pulled the horses round. The Apaches dispersed before them as they rode through. The boy felt a thousand eyes, like arrows, at his back.

"I'll be waiting," the boy heard Brannigan whisper to himself as they rode clear. "I'll be waiting."

When, at last, they were riding free in open country, Brannigan lowered the Henry from Sweetwater's temple. She turned to him and spoke for the first time that day. "You are a fool, Brannigan, deceived by your lust. Lobo has never killed any woman."

Brannigan dismissed her words and set his face ahead where he could see the tall, flat rock they called Table Butte.

The last of the daylight lent the landscape a grey look as they spiralled up the trail to the top of Table Butte.

When they were unsaddled and unpacked, Brannigan lit a fire and settled next to it. He had the woman close to him, and the Henry was on his lap. He did not intend to sleep that night. There was a slight chance that they had been followed, but he doubted whether the Apaches would dare make a move while he had the woman so close. At the top of the trail when he had looked back he had seen no sign of followers.

"How do you feel, boy? Mebbe you'll get your horse back, uh?"

The boy looked at Brannigan, briefly, but lowered his eyes a shade too quickly. Brannigan sensed something was wrong.

"Spit it out, boy."

The fire crackled in the silence. The boy spoke.

"Is it really worth it?"

"Worth what?" There was puzzlement

in Brannigan's voice.

"Worth lives. You could be wrong."

Brannigan stared into the fire and an uncomfortable feeling invaded the camp. For a long time he stared, till his eyes were glassy.

"Did you think it would be easy then?"

The boy shook his head. "No but I've seen things out here. Before the Apaches were, well, animals. Now I see them different. You sure you couldn't be wrong?"

Brannigan took his eyes from the fire and stared out into the dark, searching beyond the black veil for something he could never find.

"Nope. I saw that name written in blood in great big letters."

Now it was the boy who stared into the fire, trying to picture the future. He did know one fact for certain. Tomorrow, either Brannigan or Lobo would be killed and he knew that he wanted neither dead. For the first time he doubted his own part in the sorry affair. If he had not come after the horse he would have known nothing of this dirty business. He wondered if he should have settled for his mother's idea of going back east to a new life.

Then, as he watched the fire consuming one of the logs, he knew it was no good looking back. What he had seen, since he had left home, had taught him that the universe was just like the flames in front of him now, destroying life and people at a whim. If you were marked out death would find you. It was no respecter of persons. He felt suddenly older.

Sweetwater's voice broke into his thoughts.

"It is a sickness," she announced, pointing at Brannigan. "Brannigan is sick. I have seen the same sickness amongst the whites who look for gold in our land. He is blinded by his sickness."

"Johnson said something like that," the boy mused, surprised by the uncharacteristic flow of words from Sweetwater. She was looking at him, studying him carefully.

Brannigan interrupted them, touching Sweetwater lightly on the shoulder.

"If Lobo kills me," he said, "will you see no harm comes to the boy?"

Sweetwater nodded in half-reluctant assent, and he turned to the boy.

"Don't think. It's dangerous out here. If you think, you hesitate, and if you hesitate you're dead. Remember that."

"If you don't think you're an animal. That's what my pa told me."

"Your pa was right — back east, perhaps even back at the fort, but not out here. Out here nobody hesitates."

Sullenly, while Brannigan was still speaking, the boy lay down and curled up. Brannigan remained upright, Henry in his hands, as Sweetwater curled up too.

"Brannigan," she whispered before she went to sleep.

"Yeah?"

"Before you die tomorrow, I thank you for the Apache boy."

Brannigan looked down at her. "It will be a different story tomorrow," he said.

9

NEXT morning Brannigan shook the boy awake and gave him coffee. Sweetwater, freed now from the rope, was already awake.

The boy watched Brannigan move to the edge of the butte and, coffee in hand, followed him. The Indian fighter waved his rifle at their backtrail, and the boy saw the Apache below, making his way up the lower trail. Brannigan spat out some chewed tobacco as they turned back to the camp.

While they waited, he sat, whittling wood with his knife, his back pressed against a rock and his eyes never wavering from the shape he was carving. The boy, on the other hand, could not keep still. Like a jack-rabbit, he kept bobbing up and down,watching, waiting for Lobo's appearance.

One minute the trail was empty and

the next Lobo was riding on to the butte and no more than a quarter-mile away on the flat surface. There was no hurry about him, and the big white carried him in an effortless canter.

From that distance, the boy could see he wore no shirt. Round his middle a silver gun-belt threw back the sun's rays.

He rode right up to them, pulled up, and dismounted.

"I have come, Brannigan." There was steel in his voice as he stood wide legged before them, arms folded across his chest. "How is it to be?" he demanded.

Brannigan pushed Sweetwater to one side.

"Knives — guns are too quick. I want the pleasure of killing you slowly, close up."

Brannigan was unbuckling his gun-belt as he was speaking, and now he handed it to the boy. Lobo followed suit and drew his knife from the pouch as the white man took his Bowie from his boot. Each moved quickly.

For a moment they glared at each other, before Brannigan, again with quick movements, took off his hat and sent it spinning through the air.

"Where it lands." His words were clipped with impatience.

They walked to the point where the hat had landed, keeping well apart, each distrustful of the metal death in the other's hand. When they reached the hat they squared up, watched anxiously, at a distance, by Sweetwater and the boy.

Lobo rushed first, but Brannigan avoided the slashing knife, and the Indian had to turn quickly and face him again. Brannigan, more enraged than the boy had ever seen him, recklessly made the next charge, bringing the knife up in a long arc. Lobo, however, parried the blow, and there was the sound of steel clashing against steel as their knives came together. They stood there, all their strength of body and will channelled into their knife arms, forcing, testing each other, until Lobo, sensing no advantage was being gained, sprang lithely backwards and clear.

Crouched forward, they circled each other again, making feints and slashing, anything to gain that vital opening. From the distance it could have been slow motion but, up close, from the boy's vantage-point, the movements were animal-quick.

It went on and on. Both men were evenly matched in size and skill, and both were hardened by rough living, reflexes honed to a sharp point through lives of constant danger. At one point, Lobo's flashing blade drew blood from Brannigan's upper arm, but it was not long before this was matched by Brannigan's knife creasing the Indian's shoulder.

The frustration grew in Brannigan, the desire to be at his sworn enemy, and he made a savage onslaught, cutting the air with his knife like a Samurai swordsman in full flow. The force of the attack drove Lobo back and back, edging him steadily nearer the rim of the butte. He risked a glance over his shoulder and saw the big drop only a yard away. The danger renewed his strength and he stood his ground, defying Brannigan's attempts to make him give way. His brown arm shot out, grabbed the white man's knife wrist, and held it. Brannigan, aware now that his own attack had been resisted, managed to grip Lobo's wrist with his free hand.

Brannigan used his leg next, kicking out and catching Lobo below the knee so that the Apache went down. They were in the dust, arms still locked, and Brannigan on top, his knife edging towards Lobo's throat.

The loud crack of the rifle and the dust kicking up in front of him penetrated even Brannigan's single-minded concentration, and he turned his head slowly, perspiration dripping from his face. A shiver of disappointment ran through his body as he saw Garcia and Chato standing over them, stone-faced.

Stupefied, he released his grip and sprang to his feet. Lobo saw them now and cursed his helplessness. Brannigan turned again, raising his knife, determined to finish Lobo off before Chato and Garcia could interfere, but the Apache had already rolled clear. Some of the other scalp-hunters had Sweetwater and the boy covered.

"Drop the knife," Chato snapped, and Brannigan slowly let it fall.

The half-breed gestured at two of his men who stepped up and grabbed Brannigan who was weary now from his exertions. Chato went forward and picked up the knife. Brannigan detected his limp.

"You pay gringo for what you do to Chato's leg." Garcia had spoken, but Chato silenced him with glaring eyes.

"We take you back," Chato said. "It will be good to watch you both die Apache-style. Meantime, I will take one leetle finger as a memento, uh?"

Brannigan's muscles tightened as Garcia forced his hand upwards and the two men holding him intensified their grip. He felt Chato's knife cut his flesh and then grind against the bone before he passed out.

"See — he is like a woman," Garcia said to the others.

It was the motion of the wagon that woke Brannigan. He felt the throb in his finger and looked down and saw that it had been dressed.

"The woman did it," said the boy who was sitting opposite him.

Brannigan grunted and looked round. Lobo and Sweetwater were tied up and lying like sacks of potatoes on the floor of the wagon. His own and the boy's hands were tied.

At the front of the wagon Garcia was sitting on a barrel, presumably guarding them, twirling his sombrero in one hand and smoothing back his greasy hair with the other.

Brannigan tried to sit up straight.

Garcia watched him, the usual sickly grin on his face.

"One thing is worse than a white man, Brannigan — a Mexican." Lobo's voice rose from the bottom of the wagon.

Garcia lost his smile, his lips puffed out and he kicked out at Lobo catching him in the ribs The Indian, as though he felt no pain, did not react.

Brannigan stared wearily up at Garcia wondering how God could have made anybody so ugly. Then his eyes drifted upwards to the long line of scalps which were strung from one end of the wagon to the other. He registered, as he looked along, that almost all were white men's and white women's, and then as his eyes began to move away they were dragged back and riveted by the flare of red and yellow.

"What's the matter?" the boy asked, disturbed by the intensity of Brannigan's stare.

But there was no reply. He just sat, as the wagon rolled on, suspicions crowding into his mind, vying for room where previously there had only been immovable conviction.

Rarely had he come across that precise red colour, the rich red his wife's ancestors had brought from Ireland a generation ago and passed on to their child. Then there was the ribbon, yellow, the colour his wife had always used, and the hair hanging, almost mockingly, before him now had a yellow ribbon attached. No matter how he looked at it, that scalp was as near to being his wife's as he could ever imagine. The desire to know about it burned in his mind as the wagon creaked across the countryside, until he could contain his curiosity no longer.

"Garcia." The fat One Eye's body jerked upright, jolted out of a semi-slumber. Brannigan, the brooding one, was speaking to him.

"What is it, Señor Four Fingers?" Garcia mocked.

The Indian fighter's finger wavered

as he pointed at the red scalp, his mouth trembling with pent-up emotion as he tried to form the words he required. Garcia's eyes shifted to the scalps and then back to Brannigan again. The boy, watching it all, saw the sardonic glint in those eyes which Brannigan, still staring obsessively at the scalp, missed entirely.

The fat man fumbled in his jacket pocket and took out a silver chain which had a cross attached to it. He held it at eye level, between a finger and thumb, swinging it from side to side like a pendulum, his own eyes lurking behind it, moving with it.

Brannigan was unaware of this, until, with leaden eyes, he turned back to his tormentor. The blood drained from his face as he recognised the chain and crucifix. He stared at Garcia without emotion, like a man defeated, his wife's crucifix and the Mexican's joy in showing him it confirming his suspicions about the scalp's origin. But Garcia, surprised at Brannigan's lack of outward reaction, could not let it rest there.

"You kill all those Apaches. You do me and Chato big favour and not know all the time we kill your wife." The Mexican's head went back and he let out a belly laugh. "Good plan of Chato's," he said when he had recovered, "to make it look like Apaches kill your woman — then you would not come after us."

Brannigan's anger rose like a volcano but died at its inception. Garcia's words had shattered his belief in himself. Lobo was looking up at him from the floor of the wagon, and the Apache's stern features conjured before his eyes the faces of all the Apaches he had killed on his one-man trail of vengeance. Guilt, and shame at his own foolishness, overcame the hate he felt for Garcia. He lent back wearily against the canvas of the wagon.

"I told you, Brannigan." Lobo's voice seemed a thousand miles away, "I have never killed a woman."

The boy, watching the Indian fighter, realised the futility of speech. The man had withdrawn, gone deep inside himself, seeking somewhere in his soul reconciliation with his past actions where there could never be reconciliation. He would never find an excuse. In his boy's mind he knew this and that words had no meaning.

"When I cut you loose that day I did not expect to see you again," Lobo addressed the boy, breaking into his thoughts about Brannigan. "How many lives have you, to use them up so carelessly?"

The boy looked down at Lobo. "I appreciated what you did that day, Lobo. I'll never forget it."

"Then why come back? Why ride with my people's enemy?"

"For the white horse."

"How can a horse be worth your life? There's no sense in it."

"It's special like ma told you. We were going to breed it. My pa used all his money to buy it."

"You and he are a little the same, uh," Lobo nodded at Brannigan.

"Me like Brannigan?"

"Yes, both are burning inside. Sometimes it is wiser to let things go — ride on — forget. It is not good to have desire too much or to hate so much. We are born with nothing, and every day we die a little more. Why waste so much time on a horse? This is how it ends up."

The wagon rolled on, and the boy felt fear rise within him, that sickly fear he had first known when he had watched the Lypans torture Johnson. His stomach muscles were taut with inward tension. Behind his back fingers worked in a frenzy of activity at the rawhide ropes which bound him. But nothing would give.

10

SPOTTED TAIL watched the wagon rolling across the plain. He had followed Lobo, in disobedience of orders, out to Table Mountain and had remained on the flat land waiting for the outcome of the fight, intending to remain hidden. He had seen the scalp-hunters ride up the Butte and had known that, from then on, the death or capture of his chief was inevitable. After he had checked the sign on the mountain he knew that Lobo was captive. The question had been what he should do next — ride back for help or follow. He figured going on alone would be better. That way he would know their destination and then he could ride back for help if he needed it.

So when the wagons trundled, like tired, fat old men in white coats, into the narrow gap which opened into the canyon, Spotted Tail was watching.

The sentry, stationed on the narrow needle rock where the canyon widened, stood up and waved his rifle over his head.

"Hi, Chato," the voice echoed off the canyon walls as the scalp-hunters, passing below, waved up at him. They followed the trail up to the cave and manoeuvred their wagons through the barricade of rocks at the entrance. In the torch-lit inner recesses they halted and, anxious to complete the burdens of what had been a hard day, began unloading.

Brannigan hit the ground hard but did not seem to feel it, and the others were unceremoniously dumped, one by one, out of the wagon amid the taunts and curses of their captors. Chato swaggered over to inspect them as they lay in the dust and ordered his men to tie them to the wheels of the wagon. Then they were left to await the scalp-hunters' pleasure.

As soon as the latter had finished their work, the drinking began, and inevitably this led to singing and dancing. Only the prisoners did not enjoy the festive mood as darkness crept in and the cheap whisky was passed round.

Lobo, ever watchful, saw Garcia rise to his feet and stagger over to Chato and whisper in his ear. Chato nodded what looked like assent.

Two men untied Lobo and another two Brannigan. Rifle butts on their backs forced them over to the firelight.

Chato leered at them from his sitting position, shadows flickering across his bronze face. When he stood up he turned his back and walked into the dark recesses of the cave, grabbing a torch from the wall to give him light. Brannigan and Lobo were bundled after him into the darkness.

Twenty yards back, Chato called for another torch. He thrust both torches into the soft ground. Brannigan and Lobo were bundled forward.

"Can you see?" Chato spoke from the crouched position he had assumed. "A big nest of rattlers for my two amigos."

Brannigan's face was wax. A mere flicker of an eyebrow was all Lobo permitted himself, but in the gloom he could see the deep pit.

"There are many kinds of snake, Chato." Lobo's voice betrayed no fear. "That is just one kind."

Angered by his lack of affect Chato gestured to his men, "Bring it."

The men disappeared and re-emerged from the darkness carrying a log which they placed across the snake-pit. Brannigan had still not said a word. Even Chato noticed.

"Quiet, Brannigan, uh? You make peace with Jesus, uh?" All the men laughed in chorus knowing Chato expected it, but it was hollow laughter. Intended to humiliate it died a quick death when Brannigan remained coldly aloof, as cold as an ice-cap. The death of the laughter was embarrassing until one of the scalp-hunters, bottle in hand, lurched forward from the ranks to save the moment.

"I betcha I can do it." The man's words were slow and slurred and brought forth another wave of equally puerile laughter. The man was a heavy Mexican; it was hard to imagine him walking the log even if sober.

"I'll bet you," a scalp-hunter called out.

"And me," another rejoined.

Chato held his hand up, signalling silence.

"Pedro, I would like to bet you. I will bet two hundred dollars against all your share of our takings in the last two months. After all, amigo, if you fall you will not need your share. How you fixed for that, uh?"

Chato saw with pleasure the man's facial muscles tighten and his lips quiver. The banter of the men died down. They all knew the bet had been just bravado on Pedro's part, but now Chato had made something of it.

Pedro sweated. He knew that now he could not draw back. He knew his leader, and if he backed down he could well expect a bullet from the half-breed. The others watched, with gloating eyes, that realisation dawning on him and its quick sobering effect. He was like an animal trapped as his eyes darted to and fro amongst the shadowy faces, searching for a benefactor, but finding only the hard greedy stares of men anticipating sensation. He felt naked before them and began to sob, deep throaty sobs. Garcia, quiet until now, laughed. The others were silent.

Chato placed an arm round Pedro's trembling shoulders in a mocking gesture of comfort and guided him towards the pit.

"Think of it, Pedro," he said with exaggerated softness. "Across that little space you have two hundred dollars waiting for you." All the time as he spoke he was pushing the Mexican onto the edge of the log. "After all," he continued, "it is a sporting chance. If you make it Chato loses his money."

Pedro, fearful of his leader and fighting for self-control against his lost nerve and the effect of the whisky, put out a tentative foot and placed it gingerly on the log. Chato helped him and let go. "Bravo Pedro," he clapped as the Mexican began the perilous journey.

He edged forward, many eyes following him as he progressed slowly, arms splayed wide for balance and stiff like a toy soldier's. When he reached the middle he stumbled, and, predictably, Garcia laughed.

"The bastard is going to make it," Chato fumed as Pedro reached eight feet out, three quarters of his journey, safely. When he reached the far end of the log he turned round to look back and gave a relieved smile. It was then that Chato's foot streaked out and with a quick jerking action he rolled the log with the sole of his foot until the power and friction sent it spinning. At the far end, Pedro, his back to the watchers once again, momentarily strove for balance, his arms tilting like a windmill's. Then he fell, and the watchers heard the thud as his body hit the bottom of the pit. They listened to the angry rattlers below as the snakes vented their spite on the unwanted infiltration. Chato, head tilted almost coyly to one side, eyed the others sulkily.

"Who needs a drunken bum anyway," he announced. Realising the need for immediate diversion, he turned to Lobo.

"Your turn, big chief," he called. Lobo, his expectations fulfilled, drew himself erect. Resistance he knew would be useless. To attack quickly was his way of defence. Languidly he stepped out on to the log which was now at a more difficult angle across the pit. Then, surprising everyone with his sudden change of pace, he moved out quickly and in spite of his bound wrists completed the journey without apparent difficulty. Chato said nothing as Lobo walked briskly round the pit back to his original position. It was a minor triumph, and the half-breed knew it.

"Tomorrow, Lobo," he said, "you will fight Brannigan on that log." He turned to his men, "Bring them."

When they had tied the prisoners to the wheels the scalp-hunters returned to their merriment. Moments later Lobo heard a sobbing noise from Brannigan's direction.

"Scared, Brannigan?" he hissed. But no reply came. He found it a great wonder that this warrior should be crying. It was not befitting such a fighter and not manly in Apache eyes. The ways of the White Eyes were truly strange.

He could not have guessed that Brannigan's mind was still in turmoil from shock. The guilt lay heavy on him, playing on his nerve. He was like a man at the end of a long dark tunnel and had seen light momentarily before the tunnel had collapsed again. He fought for some clarity amongst the misty clouds of guilt, and through the clouds, like evil spirits haunting him, the vile laughing faces of Garcia and Chato advanced and receded until finally they settled as clearly and malignantly in his mind as Lobo's had been. All the grim relentless determination that had seen him through the dangerous years focused now on those two devils. The old, stomach-churning hate he once had felt for Lobo kept his mind from collapsing.

11

DARKNESS fell as Spotted Tail climbed cat-like up the Needle Rock, his senses alert. He intended to eliminate the problem of the sentry.

Occasionally he stopped to listen, then continued his relentless climb until he reached the top. Once there, he spotted the sentry who was cleaning his rifle. Gripping an outcrop of rock with one hand for balance, Spotted Tail withdrew his tomahawk from his belt with the other. His throwing arm recoiled behind his shoulder and stayed there, poised, while he judged his distance. A sharp muscular exertion and the weapon hurtled smoothly through the air and bit into the sentry's back. He let out a short sharp cry, hunched forward, tried to pull the grotesque blade from his back and then fell forward silently. Without delay Spotted Tail began his descent.

At the barricade of rocks which protected the cave he slowed down and edged forward. He saw the red glow of their fire and heard an intermittent crackling as sparks jumped out, but otherwise it was silent.

Then, adjusting to the firelight, he saw that the scalp-hunters were asleep and the prisoners were tied to the wagon wheels. Abandoning caution and figuring there was no alternative way, he tiptoed through the group of sleeping men towards the wagons.

Lobo saw him coming as did the boy and Sweetwater. Brannigan stared at his looming figure as though he could see through him.

Spotted Tail's sharp knife made easy work of the ropes which bound the prisoners. Lobo stood up and rubbed his wrists. Only Brannigan remained bound, but Lobo made signs which indicated he wanted him to be freed as well. Spotted Tail obliged, wondering about his chief's reasoning.

As the Apaches and the boy made to go Brannigan remained seated. To the Indians he seemed like a medicine man in a trance under the influence of some great potion. The boy saw the blank features, turned back and bent over the Indian fighter to see if he could help. But it appeared that Brannigan's will had finally broken. The youngster, puzzled, looked at Lobo for help, but the latter was growing impatient and beckoned the boy to get moving. To leave Brannigan, he felt, was disloyal, but there was no time to think. The scalp-hunters could waken at any time, so he followed the Apaches reluctantly, depressed at leaving his friend.

Unseen, the four escapees reached the remuda which was not picketed. They worked their way through and selected four, unshod Indian ponies which they led out. Their expertise reminded the boy of the way they had stolen his white stallion; it seemed an age ago now.

They led the horses well clear before they mounted. No scalp-hunter heard the dull thud of the unshod feet as they spurred their ponies into a gallop; they were safe.

Riding through the night, back to Lobo's camp, each Apache knew it would not be long before Lobo's band would be riding the same trail again, but this time back to the cave to take vengeance.

Meanwhile, Brannigan had recovered some semblance of his wit. Realising now that he was free, he stretched his aching arms and looked blearily around him. Staggering to his feet, he peered into the recesses of the cave and retreated falteringly towards them.

A plan was forming in his mind, and as he walked he peeled off his buckskin shirt. In the light of a single torch which was wedged into a crevice, he ripped off the leather strips decorating the garment and tied them together. Then, taking the torch, he continued his retreat further into the cave.

Finding the snake-pit, he halted and gathered himself. Then, when he was ready, he jumped into the pit, allowing his knees to give as he hit the ground, all the time expecting to feel a rattler strike him. With perspiration running down his body he moved the torch round looking for the snakes. Each rock or piece of wood held hidden menace as the light fell on it.

When he found the rattlers tangled together, he was surprised at how harmless they looked; but he knew he could disturb them only at his peril. There were simply too many of them for comfort.

However, to one side lay a big rattler on its own, and he turned his attention there. With his shirt held out in front of him and the leather strip in the other hand he approached it, struggling to control the nerves which made his arms shake. One eye he kept warily on the other rattlers.

When his shirt was directly overhead, he plunged it downwards on to the rattler, feeling through the material for its neck to check the venomous tongue. He found the grip he was seeking and lifted the creature. His fingers worked double time, tying the loose ends of the shirt together with the leather strip. When he finished he had it prisoner.

Swinging his arm he hoisted the bundle out of the pit and prepared to get out himself. He retreated several steps and ran at one wall. His leap gave him a hand-grip and he pulled himself up and out. Phase one of his plan had been completed successfully.

He made it back to the wagons holding out his snake-bag, and having checked that he was unobserved clambered over the tailboard of the nearest wagon, landing softly on some sacks of flour. He began to grope round in the dark.

"Gotcha," he said aloud as he found the case of dynamite he had noticed earlier. "This'll mean the end of you, Chato."

Having found a convenient piece of metal, he excitedly levered the top off the case and took out several sticks of dynamite. Emitting a crazy laugh he began to tie them to a piece of the leather twine he still retained, spacing them out as he did so. When he had finished he tied the bandolero of dynamite round his chest. Ready to put the next part of his plan into action, he slithered over the tail-board, holding the snake in one hand and using the other to support himself. A walking bundle of potential danger, he moved towards the sleeping scalp-hunters.

Garcia turned over and wriggled his nose as though he sensed in his dream that Brannigan was standing over him. Brannigan smiled a self-satisfied smile and shook the Mexican roughly.

"Madre de Christos," Garcia cursed as he realised it was Brannigan's face leering down at him. His hand moved above his head to where his holster lay, but Brannigan acted quicker, thrusting the bag forward and releasing the rattler. Garcia froze and his eyes bulged as the snake slid up his chest.

Then its tongue flickered and he felt a stab of pain in his neck. The child-like scream he emitted told Brannigan his job was done.

"An eye for an eye and a snake for a snake," Brannigan muttered to himself as he stole lithely across to the fire and picked up a smouldering piece of wood.

"That's Brannigan or I'm seeing things," he heard one scalp-hunter shout. They were all sitting up in their blankets now, searching for their guns, awakened by Garcia's scream as he lurched out of the cave. Brannigan heard the clicks of their gun-hammers when they levelled their weapons at him, restrained only by their surprise at finding him so blatantly standing in the midst of them.

Something in his stance, contemptuously defying them, something outside their cowards' minds, stopped them filling him with lead.

"That's dynamite, ain't it?" someone shouted, pointing at Brannigan's home-made bandolero.

"Got it tied round him, the fool," another wide-eyed one remarked, half puzzled and half afraid.

Chato stood up quickly and pieced together what had happened. He guessed immediately Brannigan's purpose in tying the dynamite to his body. Unsure of the Indian fighter he decided trying to humour him. He looked over to Garcia who was rolling around in the dust at the mouth of the cave, clutching his throat.

"Huh, so you got the grease," he grunted, jerking a thumb at the Mexican. "You do Chato a big favour and you got us all cold now." He paused and went on, more edge in his voice, "Mebbe you should ride out now. We give you a horse and you go away with all that dynamite."

Brannigan spat into the dust and eyed Chato steadily until the half-breed looked away, shuffling his feet like some errant schoolchild.

"Get over here." Brannigan uttered each word slowly, emphasising it, figuring that Chato's nerve was shaky.

Chato shrugged his shoulders, feigning indifference, but afraid of the dynamite.

"Here, scum," Brannigan ordered, pointing his index finger at the ground in front of him, moving the torch flame nearer to the dynamite as he spoke.

Chato ambled towards him and stopped a yard away. It crossed his mind to rush the Indian fighter, but thought better of it. If he miscalculated his rush he would be blown sky high.

Brannigan pushed one of Chato's shoulders hard so that he spun round to face the encircling scalp-hunters.

"We're walking out," he said. "Nobody stops us or we all get blown up and there'll be a hot day in hell to pay."

"He's bluffing," someone muttered.

Brannigan turned in his direction and in reply moved the flame nearer to the fuse. The cord flared into life as he made contact, and the scalp-hunters hit the dirt, nerves tingling with horrific anticipation. Chato backed away slowly.

Brannigan grinned as he shook the flame out.

The scalp-hunters rose slowly, like supplicants from prayer. Brannigan felt their hate emanating towards him in the eerie silence which followed.

Nobody followed him when he prodded Chato forward with a rifle he had picked up. They knew he meant business. As he passed Garcia, Chato heard the Mexican's death-rattle.

They walked for what seemed an eternity, the heat of the sun drawing the sweat out of them. Occasionally Brannigan prodded Chato in the back with his rifle to let him know he was there and wouldn't be caught off guard. When the half-breed stumbled and fell a boot in the ribs took the breath out of him but forced him to his feet to carry on. Brannigan was enjoying the role of the aggressor, so tired was he of being pushed around. He figured he was heading in the right direction for Lobo's camp. Feeling his guilt strongly, he wanted to make up for the vengeance he had taken on the Apache. Presenting Lobo with the half-breed might, he felt, help a little.

It was around midday when Lobo's men spotted the two figures and, changing direction, galloped towards them. They reined in about twenty yards ahead of Brannigan and Chato. The boy, astride his big white and riding next to Lobo, was relieved to see Brannigan.

The latter kept coming towards the stationary Apaches, pushing Chato along. He halted in front of Lobo and grabbing the half-breed by the hair forced him to his knees. Chato kept his face in the dust, but the vein pulsating violently in his neck betrayed his fear.

Brannigan looked up into Lobo's eyes and an unspoken understanding passed between them. Then, without a word, the white man turned away and began walking in the direction from which he had come.

One of the Apaches raised his rifle

and looked at Lobo, but his chief's slow, negative nod of the head denied him.

Puzzled by Brannigan's behaviour, the boy kicked the big white in the flanks and rode after him. Coming alongside him he slowed the horse to a walk.

"I'm sorry I left you, Brannigan," he said plaintively.

"You did right, kid. You had no choice," Brannigan replied, not slackening pace.

"Where are you going now? Aren't you coming back?"

Brannigan ignored the question and kept walking.

"Go back to Lobo, kid. He'll see you all right."

"But you can't stay out here. Can you, Brannigan?"

"Yes I can," the Indian fighter replied, coming to a dead halt. Then softer. "Listen, kid. You did well and I'm pleased I knew you, but I can't go back now. People would laugh and point and say, 'There's that crazy feller; killed all those Apaches for nuthing.' One thing I've learned, and that is that they're not so different, mebbe better than us. Lobo had every right to kill me, but he didn't."

"You're really gonna stay out here?" the boy enquired.

"Yup, and I'll be all right too. I've always had a hankering for the wide-open spaces."

Brannigan held his hand up, and the boy took it. They shook hands, and Brannigan turned and walked off out of the boy's life.

The youngster watched his diminishing figure, sensing that an important part of his youth was fading away with Brannigan. He remembered how clear-cut the issues had seemed to him when he had set out to find his horse. Life had been drawn in black and white. Then Brannigan, and Lobo too, had come along and shattered the delicate image he had of the world and of justice and injustice. Never again, as long as he lived, would he judge issues and men superficially.

He spun his horse round and headed back to the Apaches. Tomorrow he would ride home.

THE END

Other titles in the Linford Western Library:

TOP HAND
Wade Everett

The Broken T was big. But no ranch is big enough to let a man hide from himself.

GUN WOLVES OF LOBO BASIN
Lee Floren

The Feud was a blood debt. When Smoke Talbot found the outlaws who gunned down his folks he aimed to nail their hide to the barn door.

SHOTGUN SHARKEY
Marshall Grover

The westbound coach carrying the indomitable Larry and Stretch headed for a shooting showdown.

FIGHTING RAMROD
Charles N. Heckelmann

Most men would have cut their losses, but Frazer counted the bullets in his guns and said he'd soak the range in blood before he'd give up another inch of what was his.

LONE GUN
Eric Allen

Smoke Blackbird had been away too long. The Lequires had seized the Blackbird farm, forcing the Indians and settlers off, and no one seemed willing to fight! He had to fight alone.

THE THIRD RIDER
Barry Cord

Mel Rawlins wasn't going to let anything stand in his way. His father was murdered, his two brothers gone. Now Mel rode for vengeance.

ARIZONA DRIFTERS
W. C. Tuttle

When drifting Dutton and Lonnie Steelman decide to become partners they find that they have a common enemy in the formidable Thurston brothers.

TOMBSTONE
Matt Braun

Wells Fargo paid Luke Starbuck to outgun the silver-thieving stagecoach gang at Tombstone. Before long Luke can see the only thing bearing fruit in this eldorado will be the gallows tree.

HIGH BORDER RIDERS
Lee Floren

Buckshot McKee and Tortilla Joe cut the trail of a border tough who was running Mexican beef into Texas. They stopped the smuggler in his tracks.

BRETT RANDALL, GAMBLER
E. B. Mann

Larry Day had the choice of running away from the law or of assuming a dead man's place. No matter what he decided he was bound to end up dead.

THE GUNSHARP
William R. Cox

The Eggerleys weren't very smart. They trained their sights on Will Carney and Arizona's biggest blood bath began.

THE DEPUTY OF SAN RIANO
Lawrence A. Keating and Al. P. Nelson

When a man fell dead from his horse, Ed Grant was spotted riding away from the scene. The deputy sheriff rode out after him and came up against everything from gunfire to dynamite.

FARGO: MASSACRE RIVER
John Benteen

The ambushers up ahead had now blocked the road. Fargo's convoy was a jumble, a perfect target for the insurgents' weapons!

SUNDANCE: DEATH IN THE LAVA
John Benteen

The Modoc's captured the wagon train and its cargo of gold. But now the halfbreed they called Sundance was going after it . . .

HARSH RECKONING
Phil Ketchum

Five years of keeping himself alive in a brutal prison had made Brand tough and careless about who he gunned down . . .

FARGO: PANAMA GOLD
John Benteen

With foreign money behind him, Buckner was going to destroy the Panama Canal before it could be completed. Fargo's job was to stop Buckner.

FARGO: THE SHARPSHOOTERS
John Benteen

The Canfield clan, thirty strong were raising hell in Texas. Fargo was tough enough to hold his own against the whole clan.

PISTOL LAW
Paul Evan Lehman

Lance Jones came back to Mustang for just one thing — revenge! Revenge on the people who had him thrown in jail.

HELL RIDERS
Steve Mensing

Wade Walker's kid brother, Duane, was locked up in the Silver City jail facing a rope at dawn. Wade was a ruthless outlaw, but he was smart, and he had vowed to have his brother out of jail before morning!

DESERT OF THE DAMNED
Nelson Nye

The law was after him for the murder of a marshal — a murder he didn't commit. Breen was after him for revenge — and Breen wouldn't stop at anything . . . blackmail, a frameup . . . or murder.

DAY OF THE COMANCHEROS
Steven C. Lawrence

Their very name struck terror into men's hearts — the Comancheros, a savage army of cutthroats who swept across Texas, leaving behind a bloodstained trail of robbery and murder.

SUNDANCE: SILENT ENEMY
John Benteen

A lone crazed Cheyenne was on a personal war path. They needed to pit one man against one crazed Indian. That man was Sundance.

LASSITER
Jack Slade

Lassiter wasn't the kind of man to listen to reason. Cross him once and he'll hold a grudge for years to come — if he let you live that long.

LAST STAGE TO GOMORRAH
Barry Cord

Jeff Carter, tough ex-riverboat gambler, now had himself a horse ranch that kept him free from gunfights and card games. Until Sturvesant of Wells Fargo showed up.

McALLISTER ON THE COMANCHE CROSSING

Matt Chisholm

The Comanche, McAllister owes them a life — and the trail is soaked with the blood of the men who had tried to outrun them before.

QUICK-TRIGGER COUNTRY

Clem Colt

Turkey Red hooked up with Curly Bill Graham's outlaw crew. But wholesale murder was out of Turk's line, so when range war flared he bucked the whole border gang alone . . .

CAMPAIGNING

Jim Miller

Ambushed on the Santa Fe trail, Sean Callahan is saved by two Indian strangers. But there'll be more lead and arrows flying before the band join Kit Carson against the Comanches.